How

to Love

Your

Daughter

How
to Love
Your
Daughter

HILA BLUM

Translated by Daniella Zamir

RIVERHEAD BOOKS
NEW YORK
2023

RIVERHEAD BOOKS
An imprint of Penguin Random House LLC
penguinrandomhouse.com

Library of Congress Cataloging-in-Publication Data
Names: Blum, Hilah, author. | Zamir, Daniella, translator.
Title: How to love your daughter / Hila Blum; translated by Daniella Zamir.
Other titles: Ekh le-ehov et bitekh. English
Description: New York: Riverhead Books, 2023.
Identifiers: LCCN 2022050948 (print) | LCCN 2022050949 (ebook) |
ISBN 9780593539644 (hardcover) | ISBN 9780593539668 (ebook)
Subjects: LCSH: Mothers and daughters—Israel—Fiction. |
Jewish families—Israel—Fiction. | Family secrets—Israel—Fiction. |
LCGFT: Novels. Classification: LCC PJ5055.17.L75 E4413 2023 (print) |
LCC PJ5055.17.L75 (ebook) | DDC 892.43/7—dc23/eng/20230127
LC record available at https://lccn.loc.gov/2022050948
LC ebook record available at https://lccn.loc.gov/2022050949

Printed in the United States of America
1st Printing

Book design by Gretchen Achilles

To my beloved parents

How

to Love

Your

Daughter

1.

The first time I saw my granddaughters, I was standing across the street, didn't dare go any closer. The windows in the suburban neighborhoods of Groningen hang large and low—I was embarrassed by how effortlessly I'd gotten what I'd come for, frightened by how easily they could be gobbled up by my gaze. But I too was exposed. The slightest turn of their heads, and they would have seen me.

The girls took no interest in the goings-on outside. They were entirely absorbed in themselves, in their minute concerns. Girls with the kind of light, thin hair that spills between your fingers like flour. They were alone in the living room, too close within my reach. Had I been asked, I would have been at a loss to explain my presence. I left.

I waited for darkness to fall and the lights to flicker on in the house. This time I ventured closer, hesitating for a few moments before I crossed the street. I almost tapped on the window-pane. I was astonished by the ease with which the family moved about. That was not how I remembered my daughter—I was stunned by the power of her presence. I whispered her name, "Leah, Leah," just to make sense of what I was seeing. I stood there, not for long, a few minutes. Leah's daughters, Lotte and Sanne, were sitting at the dimly lit dining room table and yet seemed to be in constant motion, shifting the yellow light to and fro. Her husband, Yohan, stood in the kitchen with his back to me, toiling over dinner, while Leah passed between the rooms, crucified by the window frame, disappearing from one room and reappearing in another, bending reality as if she could walk through walls. Even though the living room fireplace wasn't lit, it wrapped the house in warmth. Gave it a homeyness, that's what it was. And there were books everywhere, even in the kitchen. The household looked wholesome, everything about it meant to evoke the innocence of raw materials, the woodiness of forest trees, the wooliness of clouds. And because I was watching my daughter and her family without their knowledge, I was vulnerable to witnessing what wasn't mine to witness; I was running the spectator's risk.

A woman in a novel I had once read was from Dublin and had eleven siblings. When she grew up and got married, she gave birth to two daughters. Her daughters *have never walked down a street on their own. They have never shared a bed.* The woman didn't reveal much more about her daughters, but I understood that what she meant to say by this is that she loved them and, at the same time, didn't know how to love them. And there's the rub, the problem with love. She tried.

They went on vacation, the woman, her husband, and the girls, a family road trip; a silly argument broke out and the woman looked briefly in the car mirror and saw her daughter in the back, staring into space. She noticed that her daughter's *mouth had sunk inwards,* and she *saw, with terrible prescience, the particular thing that would go wrong with her face, either quickly or slowly, the thing that could grab her prettiness away before she was grown.* In those very words. And the woman thought, *I have to keep her happy.*

---

*Sources for the brief quotations from published works that appear occasionally throughout the book are listed in the Author's Note.

When I read about her, I already had a little girl of my own. Leah. A spirited, loud one-and-a-half-year-old. Whispering in her tiny ears—and in her father's big ones—I called her foghorn. Meir and I marveled at our foghorn. I had other names for her too, dozens of them. I missed her every moment I spent in the studio, and scooped her into my arms every time we reunited. My love for my baby daughter came easily. Her father was also in love with her; we talked about her every night after she fell asleep, thanked each other for the gift that was our girl. Everything that I had been denied I gave to her, and then some. And she loved me too.

Everything about this baby—the drool dribbling down her chin and pooling at her neck, her urine-soaked diapers, the sticky discharge from her eyes and nose when she was sick—everything about Leah was good. Sometimes, looking at her or sniffing her, I'd start salivating, feel a sudden urge to sink my teeth into her. I'm going to eat you, I'd tell her, I'm going to gobble you up! And Leah would laugh. I'd tickle her to elicit more of those roaring giggles, and if people around us stared, I wasn't embarrassed. Quite the opposite.

When she was four, I wanted another baby. I told Meir, just imagine: two Leahs. As if that somehow could have also meant, say no. Which he did. I was angry at him for months, until the whole thing fell by the wayside. Meir crossed into his fifties, we moved to a bigger apartment, arrived at the sweet spot of our careers, slept soundly, kept up with our four-year-old, five-year-old, six-year-old Leah, lacked for nothing. And Leah grew up.

eir's younger brother, Yochai, who like Meir came to fatherhood late in life, tells me about his daughter. She was seven when he divorced his wife. Now the girl is eight, and as he puts her to bed at night and kisses her forehead, tucking the blanket around her, her absence is already palpable. She's at once there and already gone, leaving him stranded between who she was and who she is yet to be. We meet at a small café downtown—until Meir's death, we never really talked; Yochai was always bottled up around me—and when I get home that evening, I'm restless. I pick up a book and read about a woman, not the one in Ireland whose girls never walked down a street on their own, a French woman, whose teenage daughter has been in jail for two years. In the daughter's story, told from behind bars, she asserts that she was loved by her parents, perhaps even loved *too much,* and so she seems uncertain as to whether she was ever liked. I put the book down. The cover stares at me for a few long moments, I think I'm through with it. *As I grew,* the daughter writes of her relationship with her mother, *I became for her the other side of the wall.*

I think about Leah at fourteen, fifteen—the perilous years.

I'd studied her face hundreds of times, thousands, always thinking, you take my breath away. Sometimes I told her, you're so
beautiful it's crazy, and Leah would roll her eyes, her features
hardening, and I knew that with my lovestruck gaze, so blinded
to her flaws, I was letting her down. And yet I kept doing it. I
didn't stop. I refused to accept the wall between us.

I want to write about Leah in one go, everything there is.
But oh, the needle's eye of language.

I would have liked to write about Leah without words.

You see it a lot in movies. A family in a car, the father at the wheel, the mother striking in a captivatingly careless sort of way, the two children jazzed up in the back, everyone talking at once. This is the *before* life, and something bad is about to happen. A roadside assault. A horrible secret from the past. Your daughter's sinking mouth.

Although I did once see a Scandinavian movie that took a more subtle approach to tragedy. I watched it three times, wanting to make sure I didn't miss anything. The family was vacationing at a ski resort—father, mother, son, and daughter. The four of them were beautiful, and it was a plausible beauty, a beauty you could relate to as it did not obscure the fact that they had their own concerns. And the thing that happened to this family, the event that crashed into the casing of their lives and shattered it into a spiderweb of cracks and fissures, was an avalanche that lasted only seconds. They were dining at a mountainside restaurant when the avalanche drove toward them, sending everyone running for cover. It was over in a flash, the avalanche rumbling to a halt at a safe distance and the diners returning to their tables. But the blow was fatal, the damage done, because in those moments of panic, the father bolted from his chair and ran, while the mother threw herself onto her children to shield them from the hurtling snow. And it was from this, the knowledge that her husband had fled to save himself and left them behind, that the young woman struggled to recover. From that point in the film on, with typical Swedish restraint, the extent of the rift unfolds.

I would have liked to see, from time to time, more movies about lives that get bent out of shape just like that, rather than the ones that chronicle life's earsplitting crashes. I would have liked to hear about more families like ours, mine and Meir's and Leah's, about mistakes that are so easily made and yet somehow beyond forgiveness. The day-to-day mishaps. The crimes of will.

2.

For the first year of Leah's life, my mother came to visit us often, never empty-handed, always carrying containers of home-cooked food or overpriced gifts she'd bought for her granddaughter (she kept the price tags on). She would sit on the couch with Leah on her lap, clicking her tongue and rocking her from side to side, or sit beside her on the carpet and wave her hands around, and when they finished playing, she would feed her, steering the spoon to her mouth and immediately wiping her chin, spoon-wipe-repeat. I lay in wait for the moment my mother would bubble over with emotion, for her heart to overflow. That little face, how could anyone resist it? Surely, Leah would melt her into mush.

My mother helped me with all the baby-related matters, as did Meir. Every morning he would get Leah ready and drop her off at the nanny's, and every afternoon I would pick her up and we would spend time together at home, just the two of us—or three, if my mother joined us—until he returned from the university. The moment Meir walked through the door he'd swoop down and shower the baby with cuddles and coos, questions, demands for kisses and then more kisses, and foot-stomping if they were denied; and the kiss-covered Leah would laugh and laugh. My mother would take her leave no more than a minute or two after his arrival, the door shutting behind her, leaving me alone to take in the sight of father and daughter cracking up on the couch. My mother didn't want to be present for it, didn't know how to appreciate it. And I didn't know how to fool around with my daughter like that, to growl and roar, to produce those kinds of sounds, but I was mesmerized. Though sometimes Meir went too far, and Leah laughed until her shrieks of joy sounded like the onset of sobbing.

I snapped endless photos of Leah. The discovery of America, the moon landing, our firstborns. Obviously the world holds its breath. But it takes years to be able to look at these childhood photo albums and recognize the ways in which our love for our children twists and reshapes reality right before our eyes. For the first days of her life she was alarmingly pale, almost transparent—a bag of milk. An oddity. My heart still skips a beat at her bold expression in these photos, her acknowledgment of her own self-worth, right from the beginning. I didn't understand it at the time, didn't understand until much later that I'd had to learn how to love the children of others, while my love for Leah was the opposite of learning, it was the forgetting of everything.

Outside the frame, I'm squeezing her orange juice, yet in it Leah is already sipping it hesitantly from her pink plastic cup. The moment the acidity hits her is always a little amusing to watch. The vitamins surge through her, absorbing into her bloodstream and performing their magic; before my very eyes she's healing without having fallen ill. And at night too, when she's asleep, I feel her growth, like dough rising, her body burgeoning (lying in bed, she looks irrationally long). On the rare occasion that she is sick—a cold or some such bug—another girl flares up under her skin. Rather than leave her weak or groggy, a high fever makes her stormy, incessantly talkative. I think it's mania. Her eyes shine, her face flushes, and her voice drops to a gravelly rumble. She scares me. When this happens, I know there's nothing I can do for her, that she has slipped into the arms of fate. But without fail, after a day, two at most, the storm passes. My mother calls, all in a tizzy, to ask how she's doing—forty years as a hospital nurse has taught her a lot about the fickleness of fate; babies spiking a fever terrifies her, as does any form of excess, as I've mentioned. Leah is fine, I assure her. The fever broke and she's asleep.

The following morning Leah is once again giggling from her high chair. We have just bought our first digital camera, and now I can take as many photos of her as I want, snap with reckless abandon. Under a certain light, my daughter's eyes are so blue they look vacant. I have brown eyes, and so does her father. The light blue of our daughter's eyes is a stowaway aboard our bodies, a union of heredity two generations removed. My maternal grandmother had blue eyes, as did Meir's paternal grandfather. With the light just so, Leah's hair also looks very fair, almost yellow. I instantly delete the demon-like images and, among the remainder, choose the prettiest one to show my mother. An hour later, on our way to preschool, a healthy Leah is again eager to press everything. The light switch in the stairwell. The elevator button. The car key remote. And it's the same thing in the afternoon, on our way back—wanting to press the ATM keypad, pull the bills out of the slot, insert the coin in the shopping cart, sign the credit card receipt. At three and a half years old she knows how to write her name, even has a signature, loopy like a gift bow. At home she scrawls it on every piece of paper, *Leah, Leah, Leah, Leah.* She doesn't ask me to teach her how to write anything else.

I'm saying that the problem of love didn't come up again. I agonized over the mystery of it through my entire pregnancy, but the moment my daughter came into the world, I had it all figured out. On those long afternoons when it was just the two of us at home, I'd call my mother to tell her how wonderful Leah was. I insisted on telling her, wouldn't let her change the subject, refused to listen to her stories until she heard mine, found ways to sneak them in without her even realizing. To the cashier at the grocery store around the corner I said (too loudly; back then my voice didn't always come out at the volume I'd set it to): What was I even doing with my life before I had my daughter? I meant that I didn't remember a thing, it was all wiped out, I was born again with my daughter. I couldn't tell my mother such things, I would have buried us both in embarrassment, she would have heard only what she feared. But it was an infatuation, I had fallen in love, I wanted to shout my love for Leah from the rooftops, and at the same time I didn't care about anyone. I was elated, celebrating the invention of my own motherhood. The hugs, the kisses, the gurgles and murmurs of love. I nursed her on demand, day and night.

She fell asleep and woke up to her internal clock. I dispensed with all the parenting books. I sniffed her socks and pants before shoving them into the machine, inhaled her greasy hair, her morning breath, every one of her sweet stenches. She crawled barefoot in the sandbox, buried her hands in the fur of the neighborhood dogs. I ignored every rule and restriction, and insisted on laying all this out before my mother, this love for my daughter that I'd invented entirely on my own, and that bore no resemblance to my mother's love for me.

I rarely got angry at Leah. I'm saying that there was no anger, not in those first few years, or later. She exhausted me at times, and then I'd grimace and raise my voice, but I wasn't upset. I was enjoying myself. What I mean is that I derived pleasure from it, from disciplining her, lecturing her, being the mother. On one thing I stood firm: when a pouting Leah would start flailing her little arms, whipping them against my legs or chest or whacking them against my hip, I'd grab her wrists and say, No! You never hit Mommy! Not even as a joke! At which point she would burst into tears. After a few such episodes she didn't dare hit me again. And yet I found myself wounded more than once. When she muttered—not in jest, she really meant it—"Go away, leave me alone," I couldn't bring myself to look at her; I'd turn away from her for a few minutes, and she would sink into misery.

3.

I'm reading a book about a mother who could no longer bear her child's crying, and suddenly mothers like her are everywhere—on the playground, in the supermarket, the streets, the waiting rooms. I can identify them by their shallow breathing, by their voice that has counted to ten before speaking. The madness lunging into a squat, ready to pounce. In the end it's not the sticky hands or the damp, dirty skin folds, or the endless cycle of feeding and diaper-changing and tantrums thrown in public. What gets them in the end is the crying.

Leah cried every now and then, but every baby does. And she was always a good girl. A girl who knew no rage. She just spoke too loudly, her voice carried far; I often had to shoot her an embarrassed *shush* on the street or at a friend's house. Keep it down, Leah. Embarrassment is a simple mechanism, and Leah got it. Little girls always do.

4.

I didn't stay overnight in Groningen. Planning the trip, I thought it would be inappropriate to spend an entire night in town without my daughter knowing. I thought it would sully my intentions. All I wanted was to see her with my own eyes, and once I did, I would immediately make my way back to Amsterdam and wait for my return flight to Israel. Perhaps I was wary of the drawn-out hours of darkness in Groningen, or couldn't find another way to convince myself of my good faith.

At Groningen Railway Station I boarded a 9:18 p.m. train to Amersfoort, and from there switched trains to Amsterdam.

I used to navigate Europe's highways completely unafraid. On our trips to France, Austria, Germany, Scandinavia, Meir and I took turns behind the wheel. We both loved the sudden bends that revealed a mountain range or a glimmering lake-carved valley, and the gas stations where pockmarked teenage boys worked the coffee machines and hot dog rollers, entire lives that went on long after our departure and upon which we left no mark. But now I didn't trust myself. I could easily have gotten lost in thought and taken the wrong exit or flipped into a ditch. I decided I would be better off taking the train. I was also hoping to get some sleep during the ride, but every time I closed my eyes I was back in front of the picture window in Groningen. I didn't know where to steer the drama I'd set into motion, perhaps didn't understand what I'd done.

I thought about Meir, and what he might have said had he known. I had always feared his reproach, a fear that hadn't waned even six years after his death. That ghost still stared me down. And suddenly a strange memory came back to me, something I hadn't thought about in years and wouldn't have been able to summon even if prompted to recount the beautiful moments; there it was, bobbing to the surface. We had gone to Paris together, our first trip as a couple. It was winter, and every time we walked down the steps to the Metro he would say, walk ahead a little, keep going, I like to look at you.

I remember how it made me laugh that first time. How charming I found it. "What?"

"I look at you and think, who is this girl?" he said. "She's gorgeous. Who does she belong to? If I tried talking to her, would she even give me the time of day?"

I burst into laughter, it was so silly.

"Walk," he urged me, "walk. So I can look at you. Please."

We were just fooling around. I'd walk to the edge of the platform and back, once or twice, depending on how long it took the train to come.

That memory rose up on my way to Amersfoort, and it seemed so off-kilter, so far removed from the life we had shared.

At Amersfoort I boarded the train to Amsterdam. I switched cars three times before finally planting myself in front of a young mother and her two sons, who fell silent and eyed me warily for a few moments before sinking back into their world. They ate apple slices from a bag and talked in muted voices, holding each other's gaze.

I smiled at the children. The mother smiled at me. To her I was just a nice lady on a night train.

"How old are they?" I asked, and upon her answer added, "adorable."

We exchanged a few more pleasantries. I mentioned my surprise at the number of passengers traveling so late at night and at the overly lit car, which dashed any hope of sleeping. Then I left them alone and they let me be.

5.

Two weeks before my thirty-first birthday, at the end of an extended maternity leave, I resumed my work at the university's graphic design studio. It took me a few days to stop hunting for hesitant gazes. The months of my pregnancy had left me with murky dregs of discomfort, and returning to the studio, I couldn't tell how much of me had leaked out into the world, whether my face betrayed the struggle in my soul. Everything seemed to be in order; the graphic designers, my manager, everyone remembered who I had been all those years, and ascribed the plights of my pregnancy to some other force. Biological, hormonal. Something transient. I was welcomed back with open arms. Everyone wanted to hear about and see photos of Leah, and I realized right away that I would have to make mention of the difficulties—the stitches and exhaustion and nightly saga of nursing and crying—realized what I would have to say and how to temper the joy in my stories.

"It's good to be back," I said. "To get dressed, put on makeup, be around adults."

Back then, eight-month-old Leah was already spending her days at a day care run by a woman with arms like doughy sinkholes who made a point of picking her up in my presence, kissing and sniffing and handing her to me as if against her will, as if saying, I can't bear to part with her. I wasn't altogether well in those weeks. It was that unsettling period of first goodbyes. I didn't know how to prepare for it, how to miss my daughter in peace, couldn't bring her to day care in the morning with the conviction that I would later get her back. I'd walk out of the day care center as if I'd forgotten her there, as if only dumb luck could make up for the mistake I was making over and over again, every morning, day after day.

"We have to take you out some evening," my friends at the studio said. All but one were already mothers, and every few weeks they'd go out together for drinks and compete over who valued the night off most.

"Sure," I said, "it'll be good to get out of the house for a bit, take a break."

I wasn't worried. I knew it wouldn't be hard to worm my way out of it when the time came.

A few days after my return to work, my mother invited me out to dinner. Meir and Leah would be staying home alone for the first time. "Go," Meir said. "Go and have fun." When I arrived at the restaurant, my mother was already waiting for me, all smiles and high spirits; she too was buoyed by Leah's birth. I blew her a kiss from across the table and took my seat. Getting a head start on my upcoming birthday, she had bought me a beautiful coat I'd been coveting, a silk scarf, and a book. I had decided to stop viewing the books she bought me as lengthy letters addressed to me from her subconscious and, over the following days, heartily immersed myself in the new book, even underlining sentences I thought I might one day wish to revisit. *Through photographs, each family constructs a portrait-chronicle of itself—a portable kit of images that bears witness to its connectedness.* Now, every time I photographed Leah, with every cunning click of the camera, it struck me that I was choosing one version of reality among many. It would take me years to shed that feeling.

6.

I lay out Leah's diaper bag and lunch box and my handbag side by side on the couch. Carefully lowering her onto the carpet, I peel off her clothes and change her diaper. Dressing Leah like me is merely one more way of loving her. Tiny jeans. Sweaters. I've always been averse to primary colors, and keep Leah away from them too. I put her brown booties on and button her light-blue coat. We're about to head out, get in the car and drive to the big shopping mall across town. Ora, our next-door neighbor, will be tagging along for the ride. Ever since the deadly attack on the number 5 bus line, Ora has stopped taking public transportation, and since she doesn't have a driver's license, and taxis are too expensive, the neighbors help her get wherever she wants to go.

When we step into the stairwell, Ora is already there, clutching her shopping bag fiercely. She doesn't have kids and never will, and yet she seems bludgeoned by worry. From the day I became a mother I worry only about Leah, and if it happens that I worry about myself, it is only on her behalf. Which is why, deep down, I'm slightly surprised by Ora, by this blatant concern for her own life. But I encourage her and say, Ora, it's okay, you will be just fine, you are not alone.

Leah doesn't care much for Ora and pays her no mind during our rides. Ora, for her part, neither smiles at Leah nor addresses her with the coaxing tone grown-ups often adopt with toddlers. Other grown-ups smile at Leah at every turn, bid her to babble, the elderly especially inclined to this carrying-on, even old folks on the street who don't know us at all, complete strangers. Their smiles are meant to sidetrack, and I have to rush the stroller past them. But Ora isn't like that, she would never brush her hand over my daughter's hair or reach over her shoulder to the back seat to catch her attention. She sits beside me in the passenger seat, soundlessly sucking a butterscotch plucked out of a small tin in her purse, which is another thing I appreciate about her, having recently become more sensitive to noise. The grating sounds of sipping and chewing. Especially from men, particularly men who sit alone in cafés, eating with their mouths open while Leah and I are trying to wind down at a table or two away, after a long walk with the stroller. Or on the park benches, mothers and their children crinkling potato chip bags and candy bar wrappers, or slurping on orange slices. I glare at them, but most fail to notice, both the glare and me. I wish it was just Leah and me on the playground. My daughter's chewing does not and never will irritate me. Not even when she grows up and turns into a young woman. Maybe it will, a single time, when she's fourteen, sitting with her friend in the living room, digging into a giant bowl of popcorn in front of a silly comedy, munching and laughing her head off. But these will be the difficult years, the exception to the rule.

Eventually, Ora's anxiety ebbs. Maybe she got used to this predicament, or maybe her fear of terrorist attacks was eclipsed by her fear of dependence on the neighbors. She no longer asks us for a ride.

The following summer we spend a week at a holiday village in Germany—Meir, Leah, and me. A vast RV site stretches north from the village, dozens and dozens of them parked among the trees in prim order governed by the ancient European know-how of creating privacy where none exists, uniform yet distinct and entirely still—hard to believe how quiet. In the evening we amble about this RV land, the three of us, glimpsing personal lives laid bare: the colorful mats, the awnings, the clotheslines strung with sheets, towels, and the occasional bathing suit— never underwear, no bras. In RV land, no one forces nudity of any sort upon their neighbor, and it feels as though we could fit in, that we would know how to be European; we get the rules, especially Leah, who walks around with a natural under-standing of the world and blends in effortlessly. Most of the campers are older couples, sun-toasted orange. Some are aging hippies but others ordinary folk, retired professionals perched on folding chairs at the entrance to their travel vans—sometimes a frayed dog at their feet, or a reading lamp on a small table be-tween them, with a can of beer or a piece of fruit—silently gaz-ing out at the darkening day, or poring over a book, or talking with the hushed composure of couples who have told each other their big stories years ago and have no more gaps to fill in. No one plays music or moves too fast, not even the young families who have arrived with their children—one or two, never three or four—and are now in the midst of their dinner and bedtime routines, and the arduous journey into sleep. We can hardly hear the parents' reprimands or the children's complaints, can't smell anything either, no fried eggs or hot dogs, no whiffs of cooking—everything in the travel vans is done inwardly. And we don't actually see the children, only catch fragments of their thin, rapid speech. Only once, at the edge of the campground, does the sound of crying pierce the air, and a girl flashes by the entrance to an RV, a flicker of pink spandex and long hair, like the dizzying daytime flutter of girls filling the nearby beach, and suddenly a single shout, piercing, hypnotic—*Leah, komm her, Leah!*—before the girl is swallowed back inside the RV. She continues to cry, now with louder wails clearly intended for our ears. I hold my hand out to Leah at the very same moment that Meir lends her his, and the three of us scamper away, hand in hand, impervious in our unity. In the two remaining days before our flight back, it feels as though our love has become even firmer, that we have come to understand how fortunate we are.

7.

Years ago, before I could even conceive of the possibility of Meir and Leah—I don't know what I knew or understood back then—I read a book in which a woman in her seventies or eighties, recently widowed and severely ill, sits in her home in the southern part of Canada, having a cup of tea with her adult daughter, Elaine. At the beginning they are all there, at the grandmother's house—the woman and her daughter, Elaine, and Elaine's daughters, the granddaughters, having arrived for a week's visit over summer break—and then the granddaughters leave while Elaine stays behind to tend to her sick mother, to cook and tidy up her house. And now, as the two sit in the kitchen having their tea, out of nowhere the mother brings it up, such an old affair, the whole forgotten thing parceled into so few words: *Those girls gave you a bad time.* At first, that's all she says. And when Elaine asks, *What girls?* the mother utters their names, Elaine's classmates from long ago. She utters their names and looks at Elaine *a little slyly, as if testing.* The mother believes it was Grace who was responsible for Elaine's pain all those years, not Cordelia, that Grace was the inciting force. Forty years have gone by, and for Elaine all this happened outside of time—everything she remembers from those years she has also forgotten, forgotten thoroughly, but when her mother talks about *that day* and urgently adds that she didn't believe them when they said Elaine had to stay after school in detention, Elaine tries to understand.

What day? she asks.

That day you almost froze. And the mother slightly elaborates.

Oh yes, Elaine says. For her mother's sake, she pretends to *know what she's talking about. What she wants from me is forgiveness,* she will think shortly after, *but for what?*

In the holiday resort by the sprawling caravan site, I occasionally thought I heard Hebrew, but when pausing to listen I would invariably find that I was mistaken. It was another language, I couldn't tell what, dazed as I was by the distance from home, by the vacation itself. And on the nearby beach, the girls with their neon-bright bathing suits and wind-tousled hair all looked the same age to me; I couldn't tell the four-year-olds from the eight-year-olds—the colors and language had a blurring effect, as did the pervasive quiet, around the pool, in the beachside restaurants, at the souvenir stands hawking mass-produced mementos piled high alongside the crocheted trinkets, jewelry made of shell and wood, beach towels and cheap plastic toys.

On our first night there, after her shower, Leah bounced about the room, thudding against the walls like a moth trapped in a lampshade, wearing me down. The preparations, the flight, the long drive—I wanted to sleep. I looped her in my arms to calm her down and kissed her neck and sang to her, and she cried quietly for a few minutes before falling asleep. But after that trying night, the three of us settled into a laid-back holiday routine.

We spent the week playing. Lego, puzzles, card-matching games. Meir and I understood the unifying power of a family sitting in a circle on the floor—it wasn't a second childhood, but we weren't bored either, we delighted in ratcheting up the drama, working to get our daughter excited: Let's see . . . where could it be . . . there it is . . . great! And we kept going for as long as she wanted. I didn't find the games themselves enjoyable—maybe only dressing the dolls and brushing their hair, serving them dinner in tiny plastic dishes and tucking them in for the night in their boxes— but Leah was positively delighted, and even as she grew up, Meir and she kept at it, playing checkers and chess and backgammon, competing with passion and perseverance. In those years I didn't play with them anymore, their pleasure alone was no longer enough to reel me in, but on long drives, the three of us in the car with miles upon miles of open road ahead of us, I sometimes agreed to join them and at times even suggested a game myself. When it came to word and trivia games, I almost always won; I was quicker than they were, could effortlessly dip into my vast mental dictionary and come up with whatever word I was looking for; but their imaginations shone brighter, and they understood each other with a mere glance.

That week, in our small spotless room at the resort, we were about to gather up the card game and head out to dinner, but Leah begged us: just one more round, the last one. We flipped the cards facedown and reshuffled.

"Who's going first?"

"Me!" Leah cried. "Me!"

We'd played with that deck hundreds of times, such that many of the cards were already bent and stained; I could pick out three pairs by the scratches on the back, and Leah could pick out many more. We considered this within the rules.

"Go ahead," I said.

Leah matched four pairs in a row before striking out. I matched two. Meir struck out on his first try.

"Your turn," I told her.

She looked at me for a moment, then at the cards.

"Well?" Meir said, to urge her along. "I'm hungry."

Leah had already started turning over a card when she said she had changed her mind and was choosing a different one.

"But you already saw what's on that one," I said. "It's not fair."

"I didn't," Leah replied.

"Liki," I protested, "come on now . . ."

"She says she didn't see it," Meir said.

"But—" I began, but Meir shushed me and so I let it go. "Okay, fine."

Leah flipped a new card, then another, and placed the pair on her stack. I rolled my eyes. When I played, I played to win. She reached for another card.

"Leah'le," Meir said quietly, "you know what's more important than winning."

Horrified, I shot him a look. He met my gaze and said, "She knows that telling the truth is more important than winning."

Leah picked up two more cards—another pair. But her lower lip quivered and her head sank forward as she whispered, "I don't want to play anymore."

How could I bear it? I couldn't. "Sweetheart," I said, leaning toward her, "don't cry . . ."

"I saw the card," she sobbed. "I said I didn't but I did . . ."

I was distraught. I wanted to recant, go back, rewind.

"It's okay," Meir said. "We all make mistakes. Continue, Leah'le."

But she threw herself onto the cards. We couldn't continue. We went to dinner.

As I've mentioned, I read Elaine's story years before having Leah and, at the time, could call disasters to mind only in hindsight, in the past. I thought that if my mother asked me one day about the freezing days in my life, I'd have to do her the same kindness Elaine did her mother. To say, *Oh yes. Oh yes,* and unremember what it was I had to absolve her of.

That book had already been republished in a new translation, and with a new jacket design. I'd bought that edition too—the translation so widely praised that I couldn't not—but I couldn't read it, was jarred by its new arrangement, the variation in the notes and changes to scale, the new fingering, and when a friend was looking for a book to take on a trip, I unloaded it on her and that was that. But I still have the battered copy from my youth, and I thumb through it every now and then. Scrawled at the top of the first page in fading pencil are the words *Belongs to Yoella Linden.* Something I used to do years ago, write my name on things, laying claim. What a joke.

I read—and this wasn't so long ago, years, decades, after the Canadian—about a woman who grew up in abject poverty in a rural town in Illinois by the name of Amgash, and who later in life uprooted to New York, making a life for herself. And in New York, one day, she was on the subway and got off to avoid hearing *a child crying with the deepest of desperation,* crying she identified as *one of the truest sounds a child can make.* Reading about her, I was moved to tears. But had she been driven off the train by a girl crying in such despair, I would have put down the book that instant and not picked it up again.

8.

I reached the hotel in Amsterdam after midnight. I waited till morning to call Leah. She picked up straightaway—she didn't always pick up, and I'd have to wait while it rang and rang, both of us agonizing over her indecision. We spoke for a while. I did my best to say as little as possible, having grown careful since I'd picked up on her trail. It was nice over the holiday, I told her; Art cooked, we invited his daughter and her family over, he'll be so happy to meet you when you come back. She told me briefly about an acute ear infection she had treated with the aid of a local homeopath. We had become experts at culling comfort from these easy conversations, these weightless light bulbs we carefully held up to illuminate us for a few moments, unwired, unconnected, powered not by electricity but by sheer will.

I also called Art, who was worried about me. Everything is fine, I'm fine, I'll tell you everything when I get back. I took a long shower, enjoying my reflection in the bathroom mirror under the fuzzy pinkish light that hung over my head like a halo and made my hair shine. I've read about it, it's the kind of lighting used in supermarkets to perk up the pastries. I crawled back to bed to catch a few hours' sleep, woke up, got dressed, and went out. I ambled about, looking for a place to eat. History was more present in the light-permeable materials—the water flowing along the canals, and the giant windowpanes of the houses, and the thin fog that drifted across the city sopping up some of its calm and carrying it away. Before I came here, Art had told me about the polders, about building houses on the soft soil reclaimed from the sea. Walking along the canals, it is easy to forget that they are not just a thing of beauty, that a battle against water is raging all around. Even the houses' enormous windows are an illusion, Art said. They invite passersby to look in but stay out, and it's clear who is on which side of the glass, that the transparency is a mirage, impenetrable. I had been to Amsterdam before, years before, but I had understood it differently at the time. And the city *was* different—Leah and I had strolled its streets together, and everything it presented and everything it had to offer had been presented and offered to me and her both. Now I wandered around until the sun started to set and the city sealed itself off. I decided to forgo the restaurant. At a corner store I bought crackers, cheese, and a few pieces of fruit, then spent the remaining time before my flight in my hotel room, in complete repose.

It was only later, on the plane, making my way home, that I reasoned: had my daughter been just a little more bruised, had life rejected her out of hand, I could have taken care of her. I would cradle her in my arms, intuit her needs, and remain composed; I would stroke her cheek and soothe her and brush her hair and open her bedroom blinds and close them each dawn and each dusk; and I thought that I could want this, could wish for her to stagger just a little closer toward the soul's abyss, and I thought, well, then, there it is. Here you are.

Then I thought about my little granddaughters. I wondered whether I knew the books they liked, and whether, when their parents read to them, they felt as though those stories were written just for them, felt that they articulated their deepest desires and lent words to their secrets. My entire childhood I'd taken refuge in books, and so had Leah, until one day out of the blue she called it quits, had had her fill of books and stories and proceeded to concern herself with nothing but music, countless hours of music on her headphones without so much as a word, taking leave of her other senses. Now I worried that I was going too far again, that I was thinking about my granddaughters too much, that I was making the same old mistakes. I fell asleep, slumping into an arid airplane slumber, and when I woke up I thought, that's not true, I was never that impaired, I always understood what was happening around me, I stopped myself in time, and if I overstepped, if I leaned on my daughter, it was only when I knew she could shoulder it. Over the loudspeaker the captain announced preparations for landing. I felt sane again, and also that I had been wronged.

9.

few days following my return from Holland, Yochai
called me. After Meir died, he'd started calling every
so often, and we would meet for coffee or a quick bite.
It was clear that I had come to mean more to him than I had
before; that Meir, who had stood between us in life, was now
bringing us together in death. We met that evening. I told him
about Leah, where she was traveling in the Far East, the ear infection, the local Tibetan doctor. He told me about his daughter,
who had lately begun to favor his home over her mother's. "She
calls me in tears," he said. "It's awful." "Danit calls you crying?"
I gasped. "No, not Danit, Ruth. Ruthie calls. Danit is torturing
her. Nothing Ruthie does is good enough for her, it's like she
doesn't stand a chance." He paused. "She asked me to try to talk
to Danit," he said, "to play peacemaker."

I smiled at him. He'd had a miserable divorce. Ruth might
be bidding for his sympathy now, when she needed his help, but
during their marriage she was a real piece of work.

"You're a good man, Yochai," I said, and then he sat up and
announced, "I always thought you were a great mom." That
took me by surprise. Up until Meir died I'd thought Yochai was

irritated by me, every time we'd met it felt like there were strong words teetering at the edge of his tongue and left unsaid.

I repaid him the kindness. "Right back at you, Yochai," I said. "You're a great dad."

By the time I got home that night, Art was already asleep. I was surprised he hadn't waited up for me, but then I remembered he had woken up that morning with a bad cold. I turned off the bedside lamp, and in the darkness, the house's Northern Lights, its incidental lights, lit it up from the rear and down below, like in a museum: the galactic-blue world of the computer screen. The blinking lights on the AC control panel. The streetlamp striping the sofas through the venetian blinds. The hum of a TV sounded from the apartment upstairs, but down here I was gliding in a waterless, fathomless swimming pool, life at zero friction or resistance, and I could sink deeper and deeper without touching bottom or gasping for air.

The following day, I decided I had done the right thing by not telling Yochai about Leah. He didn't need to know that I'd found her. She'd disappeared on us all, that was her intention, we had all been abandoned, including Yochai. I told myself to calm down, to stop tormenting myself about what she had done with her old friends, whether she had lumped us all together or perhaps spared them; I wanted to be able to shrug off the shame, so that if I happened to run into one of them and see in their eyes that they'd known her whereabouts all along, the lightning bolt would pass right through me and I could keep on walking.

For the first time in a long while, I felt good. I applied myself at work, and when I got home, I put some fish in the oven, made up my face, lit candles, and waited on the couch for Art. I was determined to stop scrutinizing the signs. So what if it was only by chance that I'd picked up her trail. That she just happened to have been spotted with her daughters nowhere near any of the places she'd claimed to have been all those years. That it was by dumb luck that I'd managed to locate her address, her home, her brand-new life. It was all the same to me whether she'd decided to leave or had simply drifted away from me until it became easier to keep floating to the opposite bank. It no longer mattered whether she was scared of being tracked down or harbored a wish for it, hoped I would find her and insist on being her mother. And I thought, I wouldn't have rested, I would have found her no matter what. I remembered that when she was younger, I would often become emotional when talking to her, to the point that my eyes would well up over virtually nothing, or anything, and that she was gracious about it, would look away. Other times, we would be watching a silly movie on TV, or she would read me an article or something she had come across online and found interesting, and she would say, "Are you crying? You're crying, don't cry." And I would roll my eyes and say, "Who's crying, silly? I'm not crying."

An hour went by, I got up from the couch, snuffed out the candles, and took off my makeup. When Art returned, we sat down to eat. He raved about the fish, thought it was out of this world.

10.

Shortly before Leah's fourth birthday, a woman from a service for prenatal health called out of the blue. I had been in touch with them during the difficult period; they'd told me what medication I could take, what was allowed and what wasn't, explained the risks. I never expected to hear from them years later, but I was happy to help.

"Just a few short questions, if I may," the woman said. "For follow-up purposes."

A few minutes earlier, I had been sprawled out on the campus lawn. It was around midday, and I'd plumped my bag under my head, planning to get a little shut-eye before heading back to the studio. It was summer and it was hot, there was a great deal of sun in the sky and a great deal of sun in my life. I was working on an intricate design for a conference catalogue that was garnering praise; the professors loved working with me, I was creative and meticulous. I told the woman from the prenatal health service: Sure, happy to help. Take notes, you should advise everyone to have the kind of pregnancy I had, if you could see the child that resulted from it, you'd understand. The woman laughed, if not wholeheartedly. I also picked up on a hint of hesitation in her voice—she was clearly wondering whether I was being funny or perhaps displaying a symptom of the condition that had caused me such pain at the time. She asked a few yes or no questions, and I answered. She didn't leave anything open-ended for me, which I regretted, because I was eager to elaborate. I wanted her to know how good I'd been feeling since having my daughter, never better in my life, the baby had snapped everything into place.

By the time I hung up, I'd abandoned the idea of a nap on the lawn. The smell of grass sparks a joy so irrepressible it gives way to loneliness. I wondered whether I should have told the woman about the white stains on Leah's teeth. I'd read about that somewhere, those kinds of stains could arise from the mother's use of medication during pregnancy. The funny thing was that normally, from the distance most people saw her, it was the stains that made her teeth look so white. The question niggled at me even after I picked myself up and headed back to the studio, rendering me restless the entire day.

The psychiatrist who had treated me in the past also saw me through my pregnancy, and he'd said there was no way of knowing—the birth could bring either enormous relief or extreme aggravation. Dr. Schonfeler wasn't the type who indulged his patients with half-full glasses. He fell back on numbers and percentages without mercy, but he had a sense of humor and a feel for the absurd, and that helped. If I told him my pulse was beating in my ear, my fingertips, on my tongue, at an impossible speed, he'd say, oh well, as long as you're not waking up in the middle of the night drenched in sweat because someone stole your heartbeat. If I told him about my daymares, that I was passing through closed doors, or carrying things on my person unwittingly, or shedding them everywhere I went, he'd say, in fact, that reminds me, I saw an elephant outside two nights ago, a little after our session, and I asked myself who left it there. None of this made me laugh, I couldn't laugh; the pregnancy I'd so eagerly waited for had invaded me, the thing growing within me was closer to me than myself, was actually inside me, and yet was alien in every respect. But the humor did ultimately have a calming effect. Nothing I said seemed to faze Dr. Schonfeler, and with time I began to rely on the notion that I could not destabilize him.

After Leah was born, I forgot everything. The pregnancy, the delivery, all that came before. My motherhood expressed itself in the eradication of everything that preceded it. I didn't remember what I had planned, expected, or was afraid of; now I was no longer afraid of anything, didn't waver or worry. Maybe I was a little apprehensive about leaving the maternity ward. My daughter and I were on an island of serenity secured by nurses who understood everything about my situation. I told them I was sore and they knew how sore. I told them I was hot and they knew how hot. I worried my daughter was too pale, and they said, she's perfectly fine. They knew and understood everything about my exhaustion. I didn't want to leave. But when we did finally return home, four days after Leah was born, I didn't regret it. The island migrated with us. It would take a long time for the thoughts to return, along with the apprehensions, the connections my mind had made behind my back. I began to remember.

———

"How would you describe her appetite?" the woman from the prenatal service asked. "Is she an active child? Does she cry a lot? How is her sleep?"

"As sound as a sack of rice," I said.

The woman gave a chuckle. It seemed that we were done here.

"I appreciate your taking the time, thank you."

"No, thank *you*."

"All the best."

"To you too."

It was already some while after her first birthday that Leah suddenly began to cry a lot at night. We were new parents, and we wanted to make our own mistakes; we let her sleep with us once, twice, essentially tempting her. Even as we tried to put her in her own bed, near ours, we were telling her with our touch, our breath, our thoughts, not to acquiesce, to put up a fight, until finally we could concede. She was already three years and three months by the time I fixed up the room that had been waiting for her, laying out the new sheets I had bought and washed. "Tonight you'll sleep here," I told her. That's all it took. But the first few days of preschool were bitter. Throat-scraping sobs and hunger strikes. When I came to pick her up on the fourth day, she was asleep. She's been sleeping for two hours, the teacher said, she was beat. I was happy. She's calming down, I thought, relaxing into the new setting. I told the teacher, don't wake her up, I'm in no hurry, I'll wait. I sat down on the mattress next to my daughter and let another hour go by. Eventually, I slid my hand over her hair and she stirred awake and melted into my arms. It was only in the middle of the night, waking up with a start, that the horrible realization dawned on me—my daughter's extended, heavyweight sleep was anything but relaxation. It was a flight from reality. But by morning I'd shaken off the dread of motherhood, and when we arrived at preschool the following day, I didn't dally. I said goodbye and didn't turn around when she broke into tears. The teacher later told me that she calmed down in no time.

11.

Before I became a mother, perhaps I didn't understand how girls are loved. I mean, how to love them. I had heard about the arcane forces that make mothers omnipotent; I had read in the papers about a woman who lifted a car with her bare hands to pull her daughter out from under it, and a woman who clutched her baby girl in her arms for two whole days as they clung to a piece of driftwood in the ocean, and a woman who killed the person who'd hurt her daughter, and I knew that a mother's love could be savage and unbridled—it was the journey of everyday love that I didn't understand. And then I did. Leah was born, and I understood.

Only once did I strike her. I grabbed her arm hard until I realized that that had been my intention, to hurt her, that I had struck her without either of us being able to know she'd been struck, cheating us even out of this. But she had made me so angry, wouldn't sit still on the little stool in the bathroom for me to brush her teeth, got up and sat back down, stood up and laughed and said, "first potty," "first water," "more water." "Enough!" I yelled. "We're done!" And I gripped her arm hard and looked her in the eye and shouted—surprising even myself—"We're done!

Done! If you want me to brush your teeth you come here, sit still, open your mouth and wait for me. Do you understand? Do you?!" She didn't move. She stood there without breathing and without opening her mouth. I asked again, stunned by the whole thing, "Do you understand me?!" and she sat down and opened her mouth slowly. But when I crouched in front of her, holding the toothbrush, she pursed her lips again, reached out, touched my cheek and said, "But first I want to see your eyes." And by this I understood that my daughter knew when I was gone and would always know how to call me back.

A short time later, I began to feel enervated again. It felt almost flu-like at first, but I knew what was going on; the previous times had left me alert to the slightest swing. I holed up in my bedroom, and four-year-old Leah would burst in, climb up on the bed and smash herself into me, and I'd think, today I will get up on my feet, and then I'd sniff her and snuggle and know what I had to do, but not a moment later I was desperate again. To be the mother, I had to think about her nonstop, and I couldn't muster the energy. The writhing weight of her. Her sticky skin. The gurgly rasp of her voice. And she always came home from kindergarten hungry, it never ended. Always eager to talk and tell and persuade. Too much. It was too much. And because of it, because of her loud voice, I'd say— I didn't shout, it takes energy to shout—I'd say, stop talking, Leah, I can't take it anymore, leave me alone. My mother waited for her outside my room, I could hear her puttering around in the kitchen and then padding over to the bedroom in her nursing clogs. "Come here, Leah'le, come to Grandma." And I would ease Leah off me, and she, who from a heavy toddler had turned into such a scrawny girl, alarming in her weightlessness like a papier-mâché doll, would keep staring at me with a look of amusement, we're just playing. My mother stood in the doorway—never crossing the threshold if she didn't have to—and reiterated, "Come here, Leah'le, let your mother rest." And sometimes she would say, "Leah'le, remember when you had the flu? We don't want you to catch it again."

During those weeks, Meir made sure to come home earlier. He and my mother were courteous to each other, they found ways, but I knew it wouldn't last long, that Leah was looked after and cared for but soon the cracks would widen, and so it was crucial that I get back on my feet, and a few weeks later, I did.

12.

Leah was still in kindergarten when she learned to read, and she never looked back—she read every street sign, brochure, disclaimer, nutrition label, and package insert. A staggering accretion of fine-print warnings swept and sapped her attention; everything was of vital importance, every remote possibility primed to happen. She didn't mean to wear me down, I understood the compulsion. Food colorings, allergens, side effects, requirements and restrictions and cautions, how easily your whole life can turn upside down—she brought this to Meir's and my attention every waking moment, and if Meir and I brushed aside her worries, she would burst into tears. I suggested methods of categorizing her concerns, but that only fed the compulsion, she saw through them, thought them misguided and complacent, outright stupid. She was struck with anxiety when she detected FROM 7+ printed on a mosquito repellent I had bought her. She had not yet turned six, she cried. I laughed. I told her, "But you're so smart, to a bug you could easily pass for seven," and she shot me a look for which I still can't find words, and threw the bottle in the trash. I fished it out, put it back in its place on the shelf, and yelled, "Enough of this already! Enough!"

But I bought her a new repellent the very next day. It was tormenting me. I scoured a health food store for a natural, gentler one, safe even for toddlers. Leah read the text printed on every side of the box and gave me a big squishing hug. I ran my hand over her hair—everything is okay. Nearly everything I ever did or said to her was meant to convey this message.

By the end of first grade she already needed glasses. "Beautiful eyes," the doctor said, "but very weak." And I knew just what she meant, I felt it as I peered into them, the light blue blanketing the bottom.

Leah was still in the exam chair, head in the chin rest per the doctor's instructions.

I told her, "You can get up, honey," and she shuffled up to me and whispered sheepishly in my ear. The excitement had gotten to her and she had to use the bathroom. "Of course," I said, "do you need me to come with you?"

She went on her own. I had long ago taught her about public bathrooms. Not to touch anything. To cover the seat with paper. I had taught her not to hesitate to shout for help if needed, no matter what.

The doctor glanced over the results of the exam. I wished she hadn't said what she had, about Leah's beautiful but weak eyes, and yet now I found her silence oppressive, since so often silences were my responsibility.

I said, "I read something really strange."

The doctor didn't look up.

"Some research," I continued. "The participants were shown

photos of blue-eyed students and brown-eyed students, and asked to answer a series of questions."

The doctor put down the pages.

"And they discovered," I said, waiting for her to meet my gaze, "they discovered that the students with brown eyes were perceived as more trustworthy."

"You read that?" The doctor finally looked at me.

"Yes."

She remained silent. I searched her eyes, suddenly panicking.

Returning from the bathroom, Leah ran straight into my lap, burrowing between my thighs as if she were a toddler again. I stroked her hair; such a good girl.

We left the doctor's office with a prescription for glasses and I showed her that we were having a good time, that we were so excited we couldn't wait. We drove straight to the eyewear store and tried on dozens of pairs but couldn't decide, she looked hopelessly silly in every one of them, as if she were going to a costume party as a teacher. We finally chose round pink wire frames, and I said, "They look lovely on you. You're lovely." But I couldn't resist the notion that soon the full-scale sabotage would come into effect—that once the lenses were in, she'd be peering at the world through her gaping egg-white eyes as if somehow left behind. We spent a whole hour in the shop before making up our minds and paying. We were told we would be contacted once the glasses were ready; but Leah was adamant, she wanted them on the spot. The optician smiled. "It might be as soon as tomorrow." We crossed the street to the ice cream parlor. I encouraged her to order three scoops. With whipped cream. And chocolate sprinkles.

"It's not a celebration without sprinkles," Leah said with the studiousness of a nearsighted child, and I could imagine how she would look saying that with glasses on. I smiled at her. It was discombobulating, everything I said to her and did for her involved at least some degree of deception.

By then she already knew things that I had not taught her. Not only words and names and facts but manners of speech and laughter and body language—she had cut her strings. I was no longer able to anticipate her reactions and replies. It was wonderful, being around her was suddenly filled with newness. I laughed in earnest at the jokes she told, was genuinely impressed by the drawings she drew and the poems she wrote. The first few years of love entail so much pretending, I hadn't given that any thought until then. And she laid claim to everything. Everything. Everything was either hers or for her, she wandered the world picking and plucking, life showed and told her how; if a fruit was handed to her, she would snatch it and sink her teeth in.

"I've been waiting my entire life to taste almonds."

"I've been praying for a dog since the day I was born."

"I've been dreaming for a dress like that for years, Mom."

The way she spoke. Cutting and pasting from wherever she could. She played and tested. Tried on for size. Four years old, five years old, six years old.

I made fun of her with a fondness. Silly goose. You goofball. I was enraptured. My daughter in her pink glasses. A little doll.

Handing me her empty soup bowl, she would say, "Thank you, Mom, it was exceptional." She would say, "When I was little . . ."

A few weeks before the end of first grade, she came home beaming. Hagai had complimented her on her drawing. She said, "He's the first boy who's really into me, Mom."

"Thank god."

She gave me a hesitant look.

"You're going to be seven soon, Liki. It's about time."

She laughed. I laughed.

Without an iota of self-consciousness, she got sucked into cartoons on TV and then oozed back out of them with ridiculous, over-the-top diction and self-empowerment tropes. "You be you, Mom." "Believe in yourself." "You can do it."

"I feel so independent," she said when she was dispatched to the grocery store next door on her own for the first time. "This is the best day of my life," she announced upon her return. "I'm ever so grateful to you, Mom."

"Remind me," I whispered to Meir, "did we adopt her from the nineteenth century?"

"Stop."

But I was in love with my daughter, adored every single thing about her, it was merely a form of exorcism; the slightest sarcasm to ward off the evil eye. My daughter flooded the banks of my heart and so I had to spill out a little of my love, a few tiny drops, to keep going. It wasn't easy keeping her safe. She wasn't always careful, would come home from school without her coat (there was an issue with keeping her hands warm in the winter, sometimes even a coat and gloves weren't enough), or she would pick up a shiny glass shard off the sidewalk, or we would enter a public restroom and she would paw at everything, the faucets, the handles, or plop her bag onto the grimy floor. Once, I yelled at her when she accidentally dropped her glasses in the toilet; I wouldn't let her fish them out, we left them there, in the ladies' restroom at the mall, and on our way to the parking lot she insisted on holding my hand and bawled her eyes out. I felt terrible about it. We bought a new pair the very next day, but I never imagined it feeling this bad to break your daughter's heart, even if it was just a hairline fracture, and I swore I'd be more careful with her.

13.

I find a new way to talk to my mother about Leah.

"She's so serious," I groan. "Studies for hours on end. Stresses over exams. I tell her, take a break, go out. See friends. Have fun. She's too serious."

I take my mother on a tour of my daughter's faults, my awe and adoration cloaked as complaints. Her overwhelming need for order, her inability to improvise. "Look at her closet. Like soldiers standing at attention. Look at her notebooks." I gripe about her lack of a secret life. "She tells me everything. Everything. It's not normal." I ask my mother—what will become of her? My daughter doesn't know how to cut corners. Everything is wheat with her, she doesn't get the concept of chaff; what troubles will the years hurl at her? She's doing fine now, I say, she can still manage it all, but life, it doesn't get easier.

Seldom does my mother have something to say about this. She changes the subject, and it only attests to how well she knows me. She could have told me to shut up and it would have been just the same. She could have said, you think there has never been a Leah before, that no mother in human history has ever loved her daughter like you.

I remember how effortlessly she loved me when I was ill as a child, how she tended to me, my listlessness reflected in her under-eye hollows and the corners of her mouth, and I, in turn, knew how to be her patient. Although there were times when I didn't understand how to be her beloved daughter, didn't know what I needed to do to master it. But I always believed her. Even when I dismissed her words, even when I lashed out at her, you don't understand anything! The things she thought about me were true by virtue of her thinking them; I didn't need any more persuading, they were at the very core of me.

I had changed. Now my mother interested me in a different way. Actually, only Meir and Leah interested me. I didn't go out in the evening with my colleagues from the studio, and when my friends from art school called or wrote me, I ignored them. I had gone so far as to forget my childhood friends, to keep on walking if I happened to pass one by on the street, unremembering, and they rushed by me just as quickly—it was a tacit agreement.

Perhaps when Leah began taking dance lessons I started to understand something about who I had been and who I had become. I remembered my childhood ballet years, and that it was always cold; the chill of the wall against my back and of the floor beneath my feet, the scheming cold of the giant mirror we danced in front of, and how I considered my thighs and the silhouette of my stomach for the first time, and learned to be wary of them.

"How does ballet class sound to you, Liki?"

Now I was the mother. Millions of girls around the world are sent by their mothers to ballet class. We sat together over the rec center brochure, perusing the possibilities. Sundays and

Wednesdays, from four till five in the afternoon. Teacher: Nata-sha Kouznetshauv. I was impressed by the bold-lettered promise of live piano accompaniment.

"Does that sound good to you?" I asked Leah.

She nodded and rested her head on my shoulder.

There is no escaping the deception of dolled-up little girls, their mothers' inventions, girls whose very loveliness lays the groundwork for disaster. Their ballet outfits in toxic blue and sickly pink, their sweet slushy stomachs quivering in spandex, their hot dog–roll arms, their peach-fuzz faces. I knew both kinds, the uninhibited little girls who romped around the auditorium and the shy girls who hid behind their mothers' legs. Years from now they too will pass one another on the street without stopping, a handful of people bound to their hometown by fate and embarrassed by it. And then, reflected in one another's eyes, all will be revealed: the havoc time has wrought on their bodies, faces, hair; the marks of the adult lives they long ago stopped imagining and now actually embody, with the husbands they married and the children they bore.

I too had danced, back in the day, and my mother would appear at the entrance of the auditorium, always a few minutes early, to watch me. And I would keep going, right up to the very last minute of class, in imitation of my dancing self, exclusively for her. But she never spoke to me about what she saw, good or bad.

As I said, Leah was a serious child, battle-ready. Her ballet outfit was my mother's project—a classic cut in ivory—purchased in the most expensive store in town. Leah was the only one who showed up to her first class without tights, but we made amends in time for the next one. And she always stood out. Within every group, the attention of her teachers gravitated toward her, and this time was no different, she took what she was given in both hands and was fully present in the moment. She was present, that was her greatness. And when she grew up and moved out and far away from me, every now and then I would be driving somewhere and suddenly find myself venturing off the freeway for empty side roads, passing by small villages and forests and gorges, and if I decided to make a spontaneous stop, to get out and hike along these nowhere hills, I would always come across those colors. The colors of little girls in ballet class. A slipper in neon pink tossed by a tree trunk. Punch-pink scrunchies blooming around a boulder. A purple plastic cup buried upside down in the ground. Balloon green, oil canister yellow, camp stove orange. All the vestiges of ballet, strewn about.

14.

For years, tacked above my desk at the studio was a photo of Leah and me stretched out on the couch in front of the TV, eyes glued to the screen. It was taken by Meir. We were watching a documentary about people who have fallen in love with inanimate objects. A woman infatuated with an amusement park ride, specifically a carousel. Eventually she buys the beat-up metal merry-go-round; years after it has ceased to spin children, she purchases it and sets it up in her backyard—a scene rife with the heavy petting of metal parts. The woman swoons over her iron horses and cuddles their corrosive bodies. She seems happy, and comes across as normal in every other regard. She has a nice, well-kept house, an ordinary job (something in the nearby town, at city hall), is on good terms with her neighbors (except one, a woman who finds her neighbor's metallic affair hard to stomach). Another woman in the documentary, an Australian, recounts her romantic involvement with the Empire State Building, which began in her youth. After years in a long-distance relationship—cohabitation out of the question in their case—the woman recently relocated to New York and rented an apartment a stone's throw away from the landmark building, and now they get to see each other every day. A third woman gave her heart to a long road tunnel in Switzerland. But for the men in the film, each and every one of them, it was their vehicles. Men in love with their cars and motorcycles. Fiercely. And there was nothing they wouldn't do for them. Nothing. Nothing!

After Leah and I watch the film, we too become enamored of things and want to marry them. Mostly wood and paper products: gorgeous notebooks, intricate boxes, animals whittled from a balsam branch, mind-bogglingly weightless in the palm of one's hand, so free of gravitational pull, they instantly make your hand go limp. We fall in love with slime, giggle at the noises produced by the viscous lumps, especially those beaded with tiny corpuscles. The crackling music makes us giddy, the crunching sounds weak in the knees. "It's divine," Leah says. She is ten, and has recently begun using the words *divine, wowie,* and *goodness*! "This slime is the love of my life," I say. "This notebook is my husband," Leah says. "I want it to have my grandkids," I say. After a while we forget that it all started as a joke, and truly want to wed a string of turquoise and gold balls I bought and strung up in her room. At bedtime we turn off all the lights around us and switch it on, gazing at its cold glow while curled up together in Leah's bed, so madly in love. "My husband," Leah says. "My son-in-law," I say. "We'll have little turquoise and gold kids," Leah says. "Turquoise and gold girls," I correct her. "I've thought about it, and I wish to have granddaughters."

15.

In those years, Leah refused to sleep away from home. She would give it a try every so often, spend an afternoon at a friend's house and call me, saying, Yonit (or Nili or Yael) invited me to sleep over, can I, Mom? Please, Mom, can I? And I would hear the plea in her voice, begging me to say no, imploring me not to let her, so she could accept the verdict with rancor and relief. She was so scared of sleeping away from her father and me, in the bosom of another family's night—to her, as to me, the darkness didn't conceal anything; on the contrary, it stripped the family and home and laid their private parts bare for all to see—and every time she went to spend the night someplace without us, she would call in tears, asking me to come, to take her back. Not a moment into the conversation she would backtrack, angry at herself, at the trouble she was putting me to, beating herself up, she was the one who had asked to sleep away from home and so she would suffer the consequences. She'd say, Don't come, Mom, I'll survive, but I came, I always came, forever saving my daughter from herself.

I hated those nights she spent at a friend's. It ruined my sleep. The dark drives back home, just the two of us in the car, her face damp with tears and self-loathing—miserable, oppressive drives. We would creep quietly up the stairs and slip into the apartment—Meir was always asleep by then—and I would rush her to bed, tuck the blanket around her and kiss her forehead, all the while Leah saying, I'm sorry, Mom, I'm so sorry, what would I do without you, I'm sorry, forgive me.

Even when she was eleven and twelve and thirteen years old and asked me to get into bed with her before going to sleep, to cuddle under the sheets and talk, I always came. A deep tuck-in, she called it. You haven't given me a deep tuck-in for a while, she'd say. Please, Mom. Rarely did I turn her down. We would chat for a little after lights-out, and if she tried to tell me something, either directly or indirectly, I tried not to say much, not to ask, only to offer afterward, That's not easy, what you've told me, I'm sure it wasn't easy for you to tell me, thank you for telling me. But it was harder in the light of day, I couldn't help myself, I knew I had to hold back and I could not hold back; and if she came home from school sullen or stifled or snappish, I would beg, Tell me what happened, my sweetheart, my love, tell me.

16.

In the summer of popcorn and silly movies and bevies of friends and fits of laughter, Leah often spent time with Arza, a girl with a big toothy smile and plenty of pep. But Arza also had a soft voice, almost comically so, and when they shut themselves in Leah's bedroom, I could hear how my daughter's voice softened like her friend's. It was contagious, and it seemed as if they could go on talking like that for hours without tiring. Every so often I would try to lure them out, but they politely declined the snacks I offered until they finally appeared in the kitchen to raid the fridge, happily helping themselves to anything that was available for instant, easy consumption.

I was impressed with Arza. Impeccable manners. Spirits invariably high. What bred such a girl? In what kind of home was she raised, by what kind of parents? Unlike the previous years, when I knew the mothers of all Leah's friends, now they were the daughters of a perpetual present, fancying themselves created out of thin air, self-spawned. They came and went by themselves, resolved their issues with one another without the need of mediators, still girls but their shadows already belonging to the women they would become. That summer, I lay in wait for the chance to see Arza's mother, and when I finally caught a glimpse of her at a parent-teacher conference, it didn't seem that she knew how to love her daughter any better than I did mine, and yet her daughter was more adept at loving herself. I was eager to know if she too, the mother, was as permeable to happiness as the daughter, and every so often I tried to get Leah to talk about her friend, but to no avail. Only once did I come close, when she made mention of Arza's impossible cheerfulness, alluded to it in a roundabout way. Perhaps she didn't know how to articulate the sentiment.

That year—I remember because I caught a glimpse of Arza's arms and noticed she had done the same—that year Leah had turned herself into something of a whiteboard, writing everything on the backs of her hands and on her palms, her ankles, her tender inner arms, along the longest veins, names and numbers and lists and reminders. And why was that? Was there a shortage of paper? If I commented about it, she would shrug, as if to say the problem was mine. But when she was in her room alone and I appeared in the doorway, she would turn her face to me as if she had known I was coming, and wanted me there.

Mom.

I would sit next to her. A quick hug, a kiss. I knew to get up and leave her alone. I remembered how the world invaded teenage girls, brazenly and without restraint. I remembered how, at her age, I myself was like a book open in the breeze, flapping every which way by the tiniest gust and not knowing on which page I would stop. I understood why, at night, she waited until I was one foot out her bedroom door so she could whisper again, to herself but for me, abashedly, "Good night, Mom." I heard it. I knew it was how she had taught herself to keep us safe.

17.

How old was she when she finally stopped running around me naked? Twelve? Maybe thirteen? How plainly she would stand before me so I could examine a rash in her armpit, or arch her back in profile to show me the curve of her budding chest, or complain to me that nine girls in her class had already gotten their periods, and when would she?

I stalked for the moment of change, remembering how as a teenager in the pool locker room I would shield my chest in a floor routine of arms and fabric, how I tried to hide my anxiety from my mother, the blood leaks, the upper lip fuzz that tormented me, the asymmetry of my breasts. Leah couldn't tell the two of us apart, not yet, she showed and shared everything, held nothing back from me; anything went, which is why I was so shocked one day when she came out of the shower wrapped in a towel and I noticed, south of her stomach, a patch of dark hair.

"What?" she asked. Small and skinny. A child. Her eyelashes wet and clumped together like the lashes of a doll.

"What what?"

"You look pale, lady," she said.

"Nothing. You're dripping all over the place. Go dry your-self off."

I kept a close watch, knew every inch of her, and yet she changed overnight, right under my nose. My entire life, all around me, I had seen teenage girls whose bodies youth alone had packaged as attractive, with nothing but their age on their side, and my heart wrenched at the sight of her sunken stomach, her frail arms, her shoulders hunched over newly swelling breasts. Her changing body had begun to emanate acrid smells, which I had to bring to her attention without hurting her, to find the right tone to tell her to go shower, change her clothes again, brush her teeth. *First, do no harm.*

"Get your butt in the shower before I pass out."

"You could wipe out a city with those socks."

"Brush your teeth, Liki, you're an environmental hazard."

I exaggerated to make light of it all, and my agreeable daughter would take it all with a grin, stepping out of the bath-room and blowing her breath in my face or flashing her armpits at me. "And now?"

I loved everything about her, and thought that had I been granted the gift of being my daughter's creator, I would not have been able to conceive of all the things she was made of, I wouldn't have known to ask for them. And still I took her with me to work on occasion, to parade her around the studio for all to see, the graphic designers, the secretaries, the girls in ac-counting, anyone quick to admire how much she had grown, become more beautiful, how lovely she was, with her limpid eyes, sun-soaked hair, her face, her willowy frame. It should be illegal to be that pretty, they would say in disbelief, and ply her with all the riches of the office, colored pencils, paper and note-pads, snacks and candy, while reminding her—there was always someone to remind her—of the time when she was three, maybe a little older, and I brought her along to the studio Hanukkah party. As we all crowded around a table laden with jelly dough-nuts, holding paper cups of wine, she sang to us, climbed up on a stool and sang to us "Ner Li" in her big, booming, foghorn voice that I loved so much, even as it sometimes embarrassed me. It was out of the question to get her to do anything remotely resembling that again, standing up and singing in front of a crowd, so strong, all by herself, in her entirety; she had no recollection of the child who had once known how to stand up and sing like that, who had basked in the applause at the end; she had no memory of her, as if the two had never met, as if that girl had been purged from her by the passage of time. But that's not what I held against her now, when she visited the studio. I was thrown by her refusal to charm my colleagues again—she would barely answer their questions, no more than the mono-syllabic minimum, and if we happened to bump into a univer-sity professor I knew in the hallway, she would instantly clam up and seal all access to her delightfulness just when I wanted to put it on display. She derived no pleasure from the affection of adults who were important to me, and she refused to pander to them, whereas I, in my youth, had willingly been led down the hospital corridors by my mother, smiling at the doctors, nurses, administrators, answering any question I was asked, earning my keep.

18.

That summer, for the first time in all her years of ballet, Leah was ousted from the end-of-year recital. Which is to say, in past years she had been Clara in *The Nutcracker*, Odette in *Swan Lake*, Dorothy in *The Wizard of Oz*, whereas this time—I didn't quite catch it, she told me everything in passing, as if it meant little to her—this time she was cast in a completely minor role, a tiny nothing part. "Fairysomething," she said with a smirk. "I have a rag dress and a basket with plastic daisies." And she lifted her gaze to the ceiling and said with a tremulous plea, "Sir . . . Miss . . . My mother is blind . . . buy a daisy from a poor girl . . ."

I laughed. But I was scalded by her disappointment. What had happened? She had been dancing there for five years and had never missed a rehearsal. Her talents lit up the stage, and her body was made of dance; every time I met her teacher, she sang Leah's praises. What happened?

I slung an imaginary flower basket over my arm and, like her, looked up at the ceiling: "My mother is blind . . . three flowers for ten pfennig . . . Thank you, sir . . . Thank you, ma'am . . ."

Leah laughed. I kissed her. Are you okay? I asked. She shrugged. I knew how crushed she was and told her, it's okay, you're allowed to feel that way, and she said, it's fine, Mom, let it go. And I said, it's okay, disappointments happen sometimes, and she said, I asked you to let it go.

The recital was such a letdown. "The whole production felt dragged out," I told Leah. "Uninspired."

But she herself had a marvelous time. She chirped about the missteps they made throughout the evening, the last-minute saves, how they had laughed their heads off behind the curtain. She said, "Natasha was an absolute darling, she didn't make a big deal out of any mistake and didn't freak out about anything."

I nodded. But it annoyed me that she didn't hold even the slightest grudge against her teacher, that she so easily allowed herself to be tossed aside.

19.

The trick is not to show too much interest in your children's secret lives, I knew that. To keep your eagerness in check. I knew that many of the habits Leah and I had cultivated throughout her childhood came with an expiration date, that her teens would touch down and sweep her away in a roiling river of biochemistry, a skewed understanding of reality and a misguided focus. The tiniest remark tossed her way would become the center of her universe, the sun in her solar system—inane teenage stuff.

But even in those years, thirteen, fourteen years old, I still kissed and hugged her endlessly. In bed, before she went to sleep, I would kiss her hair and face and tell her, I feel sorry for you, I do, you'll never be able to smell this heavenly smell right here—and bury my nose in the crook of her neck. How will you ever know what you're missing? I would ask, and Leah would laugh, Mom, what are we going to do with you, you're bananas. But she was pleased, we still relied on our rituals. Or I would enter her room in the late afternoon—by then she was fourteen and a half with her ears perpetually plugged—and put my hand on her head, triggering the intimate gesture of her unplugging

herself and rejoining the world, with her slightly babyish teas-
ing voice, *Hey, Mom.* A temporary access that I took full advan-
tage of. And I would tell her, I just missed you, that's all, and sit
beside her on the bed. I missed my daughter, I would say, is that
allowed? Is there a law against it? To which Leah would sigh—
though at that time her own youth had not yet exhausted her—
and roll over onto her back and reach her arms out to me and
say, you came just in time, I'm giving out free hugs.

In the weeks leading up to the recital, the many days Leah spent in rehearsal, I was once again racked by thoughts and would crawl into bed for long hours every afternoon, only to wake up and prowl the night. All of a sudden I hated sleeping in the dark. I was afraid of the transition from one day to the next. I liked being awake alone when Meir and Leah were asleep. I was alone but without the loneliness, had not one iota of worry, could stand over their beds and listen at will. But in the morning I was spent, and Leah paid the price. I didn't hug her when she woke up, and was quick to anger when she came home in the evening. At night, in front of the TV, I recoiled when she rested her head on my shoulder, but she wouldn't relent, merely waited a few moments before trying again. I felt miserable about it. I sought treatment; I knew what had to be done. The summer I turned twenty-seven, the long months of my pregnancy a few years later, the seven weeks in bed when Leah was four—I wouldn't let it happen again. I got out of bed every morning and went to the studio, only sometimes, rarely, leaving in the middle of the day to go home. I would mount the stairs with loud thuds, jangling my keys, rattling the lock. I was afraid of finding Meir there—it had come to that. I thought about the woman in a book I had once read, whose marriage started to fizzle right after she ran into her husband on the street a town over, in the middle of the day. I understood her distress so well. She had—both of them had—innocent reasons and real justifications for being there, and when they stopped before each other, there was even something a little funny about this crossing of paths; but the marriage collapsed under the burden. Such a chance encounter, in broad daylight, external to the ever-familiar story of life. With that couple in mind, I would clomp into the house, slam the door shut, and announce my arrival into the void. But a few months later I was back on my feet, and I did not waver again in all the years that followed, not even once.

At the tail end of summer, I happened to run into Natasha on the street. A quick hug. How have you been and how have you been. I was angry with her, she knew exactly why, there was no point pretending otherwise.

"You look wonderful," she said.

I refused to indulge her. I thought, I'm not going to play along, Natasha. I gave her a pursed-lip thank-you.

"I thought about calling," she said.

"Yes."

"I didn't understand what happened," she said. "Leah had her part nailed down, she was the perfect Hermia, and then suddenly, out of nowhere . . ."

I gave her a look that said there was not one thing she knew about my daughter that I did not.

"I talked to her," Natasha continued. "I tried to understand, thought maybe something happened. That something must have happened. She was adamant, said she would stay but only for a minor role, she wouldn't hear of a principal one. Under no circumstances."

I nodded.

"But why?" Natasha asked.

"Not everything can be explained," I said. "Especially at that age."

"It's such a shame. I hope she's using summer break to rest and recharge."

"Yes," I said. "She'll get some rest and be back to her old self again."

We parted with another quick hug.

20.

When I return from Holland, Art picks me up from the airport. I didn't ask him to, but it seemed like a given to him. We have been together for a few months now, and before I embarked on my journey he asked for the details of my return flight. "I'll be there to greet you, Yoella," he said. "You're not alone."

Meir and I didn't wait for each other at airports, neither he for me nor I for him. We didn't make each other coffee when we prepared ourselves a cup. We were happy to if the other asked, of course; what I mean is that we didn't offer. Once, when I got stuck on the side of the highway with an empty gas tank, I didn't call him. Later, he had it out with me. He would have come right away, waiting on the shoulder for over two hours until roadside assistance arrived was insanity, it was so dangerous, what was I thinking.

And honestly, I don't know what I was thinking. I could never anticipate what he deemed the right thing to do.

But when Leah and I returned from our brief travels in Europe, he always showed up. We would walk into the arrivals area and sweep our gazes around the hall, worried that perhaps he had forgotten, but he always came, and Leah would rush toward him, wedging herself into his arms; and when I reached them he always extended his arm and pulled me into the hug, looping the three of us together.

21.

We lived not far from the university. Meir and I both worked there, and Leah had started high school a twenty-minute ride from our house. In our building, besides us and Ora, there were two other occupant-owned apartments—two older couples—and two rentals, with an almost yearly turnover of tenants. For the most part, these were students who, with little grasp of the night's capacity to amplify sound, would bound up and down the stairs at the oddest hours; but for two years straight, one of these apartments was occupied by the Middlebergs. They were a young, bruised family. Two small children, a boy and a girl, and endless shrieking, mostly from the father, whom we could hear almost every morning and sometimes at night too. And yet it was the mother who truly frightened me. She rarely blew up, but when she did, at the end of each screaming fit a hard silence would settle over the street, an unbearable sadness. Sometimes she screamed at the boy too, especially when he refused to get dressed or do some other thing she had asked; but the bulk of her despair was directed at her daughter, whom we never heard above the mother's outcry: Enough, leave me alone, enough.

But once every few weeks, all of a sudden, high spirits would descend on them and they would go out, all four of them, for a stroll through the neighborhood. They would chat, licking Popsicles they bought at the kiosk. There was no way to understand why or what tipped the scales each day, and it seemed they lived entirely unto themselves, by a principle known only to them. Two years later they moved away, leaving by the dumpster a few mugs, a frying pan, a plastic table cover, and a few old, threadbare children's books.

In the morning, whenever we could, the three of us would head out together for the bus stop at the intersection. Leah would sit there waiting for her bus to school, while Meir and I continued north on the footpath that led up to the campus. I feared that walk, thirty minutes of dread waiting for Leah to reach her destination and text me; and if she happened to forget, I would be paralyzed with anxiety.

Only once did Meir lose his patience. "She's a teenager," he said. He didn't raise his voice. "She gets to school, sees a friend at the gate, and forgets everything else, including texting you, so let her be."

He was right. Worry is a straitjacket, and so is love. I promised him I'd do a better job of holding myself together. But even when she was out of view, I was watching closely, I don't know exactly what. I was cautious, but it was a conjuring caution, akin to superstition; I knew that if I covered all my bases, Leah would come back. I would hear her footsteps on the stairs. She would appear at the door. And how surprised I was each time anew, not by the fact of her return but by her palpability, she was more real than anything I could remember. Her voice, smell, movements, gait. She would be standing in front of me talking, when suddenly she would start spinning every which way, her arms, legs, and hair blurring before my eyes; and I would think, this is not how I remembered you, not to this extent. Or with Arza, when they returned from school together and barged into our house, a blast of youth moving around me like flares of color, objects from the window of a speeding car, especially Arza, whom I could never catch at rest, but Leah as well, Leah didn't stop either.

I would eavesdrop on them. The ripples of sarcasm they had learned to unleash. The grandiose honesty (grandiose, I have no other word for it) with which they spoke about their bodies, feelings, loyalties.

It's stupendous, they told each other. *Positively stupendous.*

Goodness gracious.

Lend me your ear.

Hark.

I had a simply divine day.

What an absolutely wretched day. A devastating day.

Old words had migrated from the outskirts of language to the epicenter of their speech, for reinvention. And the ease with which they lavished their love and adoration and entireties on each other—

My dearest darling.

My perfect petal.

My love.

The stirring of each other's emotional pots; quick to band

together in love or hate of this boy or that girl for something they had said, for the love they had granted or withheld, for their sweetness, their wickedness.

Some of this I remembered from my own youth, knew how girls entangled one another in webs spun out of powerful and imprecise emotions; I too, back in the day, had fallen in love with my friends and they with me. Other aspects of Leah and Arza's behavior I deciphered gradually. The world reached them differently than it had reached me at their age, they saddled different loads as the internet tore down more and more partitions; they developed a cunning sense of direction and a knack for covering their tracks. I had no way of knowing what exactly they understood or how, and if this knowledge was to their detriment. They were different creatures, a new breed, and still they were girls, like all girls since time immemorial. The earth they stood on still rotated on its axis in the same direction and at the same speed, and the sun also rose and the sun went down, and all things toiled to weariness.

They debated the hairiness of their faces and limbs. The measurements of their waists. The silliness of their toes. They called each other dippy names rooted in affection. They talked as if they were the originators of irony, as if it was they who had come up with the concept of saying one thing while meaning its opposite.

"Look at me. A unibrow. Scaring kids on the streets. An ogre."

"You're an ogre? You? What does that make me, Bigfoot?!"

"Oh please, you pinhead. You're perfect."

It irritated me. Arza irritated me. I didn't want to listen.

They fell slightly in love with every boy they despised, and slightly despised every boy they fell in love with, and never left home without wearing silly bras intended to broadcast their femininity while at the same time concealing it, like in that book about a struggling woman whose life bore no resemblance to mine and yet I still burst into tears reading about the breasts she suddenly sprouted at eleven or twelve, breasts that she was *too young for,* that she had *no right to,* that she had to carry with her to school and back, day after day.

"My love."

"No, you, you're mine."

I listened to them. Kept a close watch on what and how much Leah ate. Made sure she wasn't starving herself. That she was sleeping well. Nothing escaped my notice, not the slightest mood swing. Her voice. The light and shadow in her gaze. They were both beautiful, but Arza's was a badgering beauty, a burden; it infiltrated the room and altered the atmosphere even as Arza herself stood at the threshold, whereas Leah's beauty unspooled more slowly and could be overlooked.

"Gorgeous."

"You, you. The prettiest."

"Perfect."

"The crown of Creation."

"Ha ha ha."

Everything was hyperbole and yet they would not tolerate any embellishments from anyone around them, and if I wanted to tell them something, or marveled at Leah in her friend's presence, or tried to recount to them anything at all—I was instantly accused.

"It wasn't like that."

"No?"

"Wow. You're making it out to be way more than it was, Mom."

"I am?"

"Wow."

And in front of her friend, Leah would hug me and say, "My mom won the Exaggerator of the Year Award," to which Arza would reply, "Mine won Exaggerator of the Century," and we'd laugh, it was all in good spirit. But I also believed her, deep down I believed that I was not adept at conversing, or at comprehension, that I had to doubt myself in this too. Nevertheless, time and again I would try to initiate some exchange with them. By now I couldn't abide Arza and hoped she would go away, which she strongly sensed. And for that, more than for anything, I was punished.

22.

My daughter and her friend huddle at the computer in her room, watching videos. I know what they're watching, harmless things, mostly music, shopping and fashion, but I have long ago realized that it is not only darkness that lies in wait for Leah, that the world is bathed in a beautiful white light that siphons off teenage girls' energy. They are especially partial to cooking tutorials in which the ingredients appear out of nowhere at just the right moment, to be prepared by hands whose owners aren't revealed. I place a bowl of sliced fruit on the table beside them and scamper out of the room without shutting the door behind me. The more time they spend looking at mouthwatering dishes from around the world, the less they eat.

Leah still dances twice a week, in the afternoon at the rec center, a ten-minute drive from our house. Meir thinks that now, having turned fourteen, she can get there and back by herself. There are buses, he says, and highlights the stops on a map he has printed out. I say he should have discussed it with me. I also say, winter is just around the corner, this isn't the time for her to be spending hours out of the house. We both fall silent, and Meir shakes his head. This is how we fight. In the end he says, I have no intention of continuing to drive her around, and I say, I understand, I'll drive her, it's not an issue for me.

But there is an issue. I drop her off at the rec center on schedule, and when she enters the building, instead of driving off, I pull into a parking space and switch off the engine. Every now and then I start the car again for a few moments to warm up or listen to the news. When she exits the building two hours later, her thin silhouette switches on and off in the misty head-lights of passing cars, and when I start the engine and flash the lights, she picks up her pace, and with each step she takes toward me her body drains of dance.

You're making a mistake, Meir tells me again when summer rolls in. It's important for her that you trust her. Important that she find her independence, know how to get to and fro, venture out into the world and understand her place in it. But very soon he drops it, and I drive her around, week after week, month af-ter month. The following winter is not as frigid, yet at times, when she gets into the car, she brings with her such a glacial chill it seems she has fallen into the warmth of the car from up above, from outer space.

Arza doesn't dance, she is in the choir. Sometimes, when they are together in our house, sprawled on the living room couch, she belts out a line from a song she has been practicing, crooning in comic falsetto, and Leah doubles over with laughter. Unlike her speaking voice, Arza's singing voice is steady and captivating, she knows how to wield it, which is maybe why my daughter's laughter embarrasses me, the way she gives of herself so freely and unwittingly to her friend and is the weaker for it. I worry about Leah, because now she knows things without understanding them. And perhaps this is the moment that I realize my daughter is sly. That I have seen something in her that I cannot teach myself to love.

23.

The summer between seventh and eighth grade a new family moves into the building across from ours. Leah and I stand on the balcony, watching the moving truck back up into the parking lot. A young man in an undershirt jumps out of the driver's seat onto the curb, walks to the side of the truck, and slides the back door open. He hops in, disappearing for a moment before hauling out two stools, a few framed posters of animated movies, a pile of woolen blankets, and a wheelchair. To myself I think: a young couple, two children, and a grandmother.

I took the day off, promised Leah we would go buy her a backpack and notebooks for the upcoming school year, then have lunch at the new Indian restaurant we'd read about. Unlike me, who frequented only two restaurants on the east side of town throughout my entire childhood and adolescence, my daughter is well versed in many cuisines. Japanese, Italian, French, Thai. Our favorite ice cream parlor is on the same street, and after the Indian restaurant we will stop for ice cream. It's all very easy and congenial, and as we stand on the balcony I reach out and tug her toward me. The only thing putting a damper on our day is the weather. It's sweltering.

A blue station wagon pulls onto the street and parks next to the truck. The driver, tall and slim, gets out, walks over to the wheelchair, and locks the brakes. Then he turns back to the car, lifts his daughter out—I am assuming she's his daughter—an eleven- or twelve-year-old girl with light curly hair and a book in her hands, and gently lowers her into the chair. He tells her something and she nods. Stroking her forehead, the father places her left hand on the black control box attached to the armrest. The daughter smiles, and with the slight tap of her finger on the box the chair swivels a few degrees sideways. As children, we used to look out from our schoolyard at a rehabilitative school across the street; it was back then that my mind fused wheelchairs with spasming limbs, the children and the chairs seemed one, and even now, thirty years later, I can feel the fear flare up inside me.

There is no one else in the car, no mother, no siblings. The father turns to the truck driver and they deliberate in loud voices, yet I can't parse the words. I forget about Leah standing beside me, simply forget her very existence. The father and the driver climb back into the truck and the girl taps her finger again, setting her chair into spin mode, round and round, faster and faster, and while I blink the image into focus, the father peers out of the truck and hollers to his daughter: "Yoella, enough!"

My gaze engulfs Leah, who hangs her head and bursts into sobs. But what happened, Leah? What happened? Why are you crying?

She has no explanation.

That evening, on our way back from the restaurant, Leah breaks her left arm. One moment she's walking next to me on the pavement, and the next she's lying flat on the asphalt with her arm bent at an unthinkable angle. I alert Meir and my mother, who immediately calls her colleagues at the hospital, and the following morning the three of us escort Leah in ridiculous gowns and paper hats to the operating room.

Leah's spirits are high, painkillers and smiles. It takes me back to when she was five and woke up from anesthesia after a small surgical procedure on her eardrum, how she struggled to resurface from the deep. Her personality came back in increments, the anger and confusion, the sadness, and finally the exuberance. This time, a fellow doctor and longtime friend of my mother's tries to comfort me. She stresses that Leah did not show any signs of anxiety before being put under. She says, Now you too, Yoella, try to relax.

Meir and I sit in the waiting room. He seems irritated with me, but he isn't irritated, he's just trying to understand how Leah suddenly slipped. I explain again. We left the restaurant and walked to the car. Not a second after she fell, a crowd gathered around us, people tried to help, there was such a commotion that I didn't think to check, maybe she had tripped on something, a bump or a rock on the sidewalk. Later, Meir brings us coffee from the cafeteria and we wait for the nurse to inform us that our daughter has been transferred from the operating room to recovery. On a plane to Stockholm with Leah a few years earlier, there was a young man sitting next to us who spent the entire flight staring at the seatback screen in front of him, his eyes fixed squarely on the flight progression map without straying once, not even when he ate—five hours without getting up or shifting his gaze. I wondered at the time whether it was a mental disorder, or a form of meditation, or if perhaps he had drugged himself before stepping onto the plane. Now I think he was just scared. For two and a half hours I thumb through a newspaper someone left on one of the chairs, reading without understanding, and when the nurse finally appears, I return to myself, as if it is I who has just been woken up.

We stand on either side of Leah's bed. A few moments earlier the doctor spoke with us outside her room with the matter-of-fact composure common to doctors. Two pins were inserted. While there was no injury to the growth plate, there was significant nerve damage, which might result in overstimulation across the fracture site. Alternatively, it might result in understimulation. We'll find out in the next few months, he said casually, we'll follow up, no point wasting time with assumptions and conjectures. He made a point to alternate his gaze between Meir and me while he spoke—I noticed this—and also held my arm softly to convey sympathy.

The previous time she was in the recovery room, the touching and sounds had upset her, so this time we smile at Leah without touching or talking. She turns her face to the wall and cries voicelessly. The train of tranquilizers took her far away from us, and when it was time to bring her back, dropped her off at the wrong station, at too great a distance from herself. At last her crying ebbs and she falls asleep.

At night I stay on the ward and sleep in an armchair by her bed. When I run into my mother's doctor friend again, I'm still miffed. Why would anyone put a child under while they're scared, I lay into her, why couldn't they try to calm them down first? The doctor smiles at me and goes back to her business. She's seen and heard it all, she's a doctor, she knows that no matter what she does, there's no pleasing people. Later I complain to my mother that her friend is insensitive, that even as a child I disliked her, that she is a horrible woman, that she talks nonsense, and I go on and on in this vein until my mother suddenly tenses and says, Okay, Yoella, that's enough, we get it, I get it.

24.

hen there begins a period in which I have no idea what I am about to say until I say it, and often surprise myself by saying things I didn't know I was thinking or don't know the reason for saying. But when Leah begins to recover and her limb resumes its function, I calm down. For weeks she is startled by the slightest touch on her broken arm, maybe because she can't actually feel it—the lack of sensation is itself a type of sensation, a deviation of sensory faculties—but now she returns to her old self. When I place my finger on the soft skin of her inner arm she nods, can feel my finger; not the way she used to, before the fracture, but there's no more of those unbearable stimuli shooting into her cortex through thick cloudy layers. Good, I say, we're on the right track, you'll be dancing again before you know it, and Leah says, Mom, I've been wanting to tell you, I already told Natasha.

I don't understand.

I'm not going back to dance class, she says. I've already made up my mind.

I ascribe her dejection to the enervating fear of pain. You

don't have to decide right now, I say. It's not the right time, you're in no state to decide. First get better and then we'll see.

But that very evening she throws her ballet clothes into a pile—dozens of leotards and props from years of dancing—and places them in a big bag by the door. Take it, okay? she says, meaning to the clothes collection bin two blocks away. And then she changes her mind, I'll take it myself, she says. And already she's outside, the bag in her good hand, and when she returns some minutes later, both hands are empty.

Not even once, in the year she lived across from us, did we talk to the other Yoella. Now and then we crossed paths in the afternoon as she was being dropped off by a minivan—from where I don't really know—unloaded and wheeled up the driveway. I never heard her voice, and we hardly ever saw her father either, only a handful of times at night, coming in or going out, and then I'd wonder who stayed with the girl, who was looking after her in his absence. A year after they moved into the neighborhood, they moved out.

25.

I try to remember what my life was like before seeing my daughter through the window of her Groningen home. What I thought about. How I fell asleep at night. The hour before sleep sets in is a pothole I struggle to skirt. I pick up a book I started reading before my trip to Holland and wait for Art to put his hand on my arm to let me know that it's okay. That I'm okay. That I should give it time.

Winter is over. I slowly regain my concentration. I have no plan. In a recurring dream, I go back to Groningen, knock on the door and wait. It is dark outside, and my daughter's lit house is unfathomable and unbearably tempting, as if I were a homeless person. I pound on the door, again and again, louder with each blow.

With Art's gentle prodding, we go out to plays, movies, restaurants. Every few weeks we have Art's daughter and her family over for dinner at my house. I'm grateful for Sharona's two small boys, spirited redheads who can't possibly remind me of us, and I wonder what would have become of Meir and me had we had a boy. The idea is so outlandish, the imagination can't sustain it.

On other days, after dinner, we carry our wineglasses to the living room and watch the news. Art almost always spends the night, and before lights-out, he gathers the dishes we have scattered around the house for me to give a quick rinse, folds the TV blanket, and plumps the couch pillows. Darkness requires order. Then we convene in the shared destiny of the night. In the bathroom we maneuver around each other, readying ourselves. Brushing teeth, washing faces. Art gets into bed before me, turns on both our reading lamps, folds down the edge of the blanket for me, and with his hands resting loosely on his heart, waits for me to join him. He never dives into reading without me. But we never read the same books—together in the ocean of the bed, we each hang on to our own raft, floating to wherever it will take us.

I read about the difficult, anxious relationship of an English woman with her adoptive mother. *I can't remember a time when I wasn't setting my story against hers,* she writes. *It was my survival from the very beginning.* She writes about adopted children, about the *absence, a void, a question mark at the very beginning of* their *lives. A crucial part of their story is gone, and violently, like a bomb in the womb.* But I think it can sometimes be even more ambiguous for children who aren't adopted; who talks about the bombs in their life story? No one. They don't suspect an erasure, and here begins another, desperate fight, for the right to doubt.

In an earlier book, the English woman had written a story of an adopted girl's early life with her adoptive parents. Sixteen years in a town in northwest England, a family of three in a small abode. *I told my version,* the woman writes of that earlier book, *faithful and invented, accurate and misremembered, shuffled in time*. But there were also the things she *left out . . . the story's silent twin . . . the silences* she may have hoped would *be heard*. I close the book and turn to Art.

Art closes his book too. He turns to me and rearranges the pillow under his head. He will listen, and I will talk.

I wrote to Yohan, I say. I wrote a letter to my daughter's husband and sent it to the theater school where he teaches.

Art doesn't ask, he waits. He knows that in the end I'll tell him everything. That's another one of his talents, waiting for me.

That night I sleep very little, and when Art dozes off, I turn my reading light back on and pick up another book. Juliet is boarding the ferry that will take her to her daughter, Penelope, whom she hasn't seen in months. Penelope wrote to her, *Hope to see you Sunday afternoon. It's time,* and the excited Juliet immediately began preparing for the trip. Now, on the ferry, she strikes up a conversation with a friendly local woman and confides in her that she is on her way to meet her daughter at a place called the Spiritual Balance Centre; she doesn't know exactly what it is—perhaps the woman has heard of it and can enlighten her? The woman offers a tentative reply, and if I were she, I'd have done the same. The incidental intimacy sparked by a chance encounter between two women might inspire candor, but does that permit one to open the other's eyes with brutal honesty? Now Juliet tells the woman of her daughter, who, although a young woman now, has never been separated from her for any substantial period of time, and the woman tells Juliet that she has three children, and that *there are days when she'd pay them to go on a retreat, singly or all together.* And *Juliet laughs.* What mother wouldn't laugh at the sentiment? It's funny. And with the hope that Penelope will return home with her, she tells the woman, *of course, I won't guarantee that I won't be all for shipping her back, given a few weeks.*

Now it's the nice woman's turn to laugh, but the story skips over that part. The story skips over all kinds of things. It is the narrator's modus operandi, she controls every tendril of the story, and she is Juliet's operator, and the thing about Juliet is that these months of no connection or communication with her daughter have been a struggle waged daily.

I'd read the book in the past and knew what lay ahead. I had no business reading it again, but I did. I relied on Art's presence beside me.

Meir and I never read together in bed. Meir liked the night-time, and when I retired to the bedroom, he would sit at his desk writing his essays and grading student papers; but sometimes he would nip into our room first to say good night, talk for a bit, screw. It was only during my difficult periods that we traded places—months when I stayed awake while he cleared the way and went to bed, letting me have the nights to myself. All my life I was wary of the wrong things, and with Meir too. And so it happened that we almost never went to sleep at the same time or read together in bed.

When Juliet arrives at her destination—a compound housing an old church and a many-windowed building—one of the center's staff members, Joan, comes out to greet her and invite her in, and before Juliet has a chance to ask where her daughter is,

Joan tells her something about Penelope that will break her heart.

As I said, I'd read this book before, I knew exactly what the next few years had in store for mother and daughter, remembered how Juliet would torment herself and how she would break herself out and into the rest of their lives. I remembered her telling Christa, her good friend, *Actually, I didn't do anything so terrible.* I also remembered her saying, *Why do I keep lamenting that it's my fault? She's a conundrum, that's all. I need to face that.*

I threw the book at the wall. Needless to say, in the years it waited on the shelf, it didn't rewrite itself, but the autocratic hold of the narrator over Juliet's fate and my powerlessness to rescind the verdict—that I could not get over. Art didn't wake up, and even if he had, it would not have rattled him, and that more than anything was exactly what I needed him to be.

26.

I hold nothing back, what I know and what I remember. But memory is a malleable material, meant for art—people sculpt in it and paint with it, they create with it, which is why I had often thought that had Leah been given a sibling, we would have been saved. But we were a dynasty of only-daughters, my mother was my grandmother's only, I was my mother's only; in our homes we were the only witnesses to our lives, our story has never been split between its speakers, or refuted, it was governed by our memories alone, we were alone in it, and because we looked normal, we had gone unsuspected.

I've always read a lot. Sad books (I liked my movies happy and my books sad), books about families and the way siblings traffic in facts, and the propensity for some to fight for the good and graceful in the story more than others. In every family, without fail. There will always be the brother or sister prone to reminisce, to curl up to the past and improve it. This propensity doesn't change over time, it is like your dominant hand. I read books about families and extreme cases and understood my situation. I was lucky. I didn't feel sorry for myself, what was there to feel sorry for? My parents had shown me love. My father passed away when I turned fourteen, and while my mother never offered me her friendship, she was consistent. I knew what to expect, to anticipate what she would say, want, and do. And that helped. She did not beat me, did not insult or punish. She might have spanked me sometimes in the first years, it's hard to remember, I will leave a small crack open for that possibility. She never called me by any pet names or nicknames, never. No *Yoellik,* no *pumpkin,* no *silly goose,* no *my love.* I didn't like my name. I preferred going to my friends' houses, particularly Orna's, whose mother called me "sweetie." I knew what families sounded like, my friends had siblings, there was hubbub, they did not grow up in the stark light of only-ness. And if I did invite them over to my house, my mother was happy to host them, offered snacks and didn't poke her nose in our business one bit. She let us be. My friends found it charming. Other times, when it was just the two of us at home, she wouldn't let herself be impressed by things I told her, or would ask the wrong question, or find faults in my stories. That's all. I refrained from indulging in my daughterhood and she in her motherhood.

The night my father died I fretted about hugging her at the funeral, worried about her reaching her arms out to me and crying, and how we would join forces. I was relieved that she didn't need any of that. She surrounded herself with neighbors and coworkers, who protected her from me, or maybe me from her, I don't know what they thought or understood; and each time it was just the two of us talking, there were always practicalities that popped up and sealed the openings, allowing us to sidestep everything else. She always remained an important part of my life. Always. Was always taken into account, and I always told her and showed her. I was often disappointed with her, as I had taught myself to be, and complained about her to my friends, but such are the laws of nature, they complained about their mothers too. And ever since my father's death, whenever I came home I would lean in and give her a quick peck on the cheek. I regretted falling into this habit, but it was easier to keep going than to backtrack. We both stuck to this slightly revised plot, it seemed reasonable. Only now, with Leah, I realized the peril it posed.

I was ashamed. I told no one but Art about Leah's disappearance, and when asked about her, I was evasive. She's traveling, I said. A real nomad, conquering the world on foot. I said that we had spoken just the other day. That we had spoken just a few days ago. A week ago. I miss her, I confessed. But let her sow her oats, it's her time.

I turn the light off. The problem is my mind.

Juliet hears Joan's words, tries to understand. Feels the terror of *foreknowledge*.

I was very serious about remembering the books I read. Another excess of mine.

I tell Yochai about Art.

"He's a good man," I say, "a breath of fresh air."

Yochai hesitates. "Meir," he begins, and pauses. "Meir was hard on you two."

"What?"

"He was hard on you. Hard on Leah. Often when we were together I thought, that girl, she's lucky she has Yoella, because Meir . . . he loved Leah more than life itself, but he didn't know how to let her off the hook, to cut corners, and you—"

"Enough."

But Yochai wants to talk. "I was worried about you, I have to say. It was like you and Leah . . . like you were the couple in the house, and Meir was—"

I don't want to hear another word. "That's enough," I say. "Drop it. We did what we could, let it be."

27.

By then my mother was already hard of hearing, and it was a godsend. She seemed happy to dive under the noise and insulate herself in the cocoon of her new disability, and I too would have found it unbearable had she understood what was going on. And so whenever she asked about Leah, we did a curious little dance. She worried about us all those years but had never told me I was liable to ravage Leah with my love. It was enough that she looked away, that she refused to delight in the sight of our love.

"Leah went away and she'll be back," I tell my mother. "This generation can't sit still."

Perhaps the hearing loss has caused some cognitive decline, since my mother doesn't ask any questions. She says, "Let her sow her oats." "It's her time." "She'll be back when she's back." Maybe it's she who is blurring the picture for me.

But to Art I tell everything. I tell him that Leah came back one more time when Meir was already very sick. That she nursed him through his final days. That she was with me during the shiva and stayed by my side for the following few weeks. But she had to set off again, I say. It's a different generation, a different breed. And really, I say, why belong to one house, one street, one city or country? She's at home anywhere and everywhere.

For six more years she roamed from country to country, calling me every other month—from Dharamsala, Bangalore, Hanoi, Chiang Mai. Everything's fine, she's fine. How are you, Mom? Only later did I learn that she was in Holland the whole time, not that far away. Not the farthest. But when I tell all this to Art, I can already affirm that everything I ever did, I did out of love.

I cry in front of him. Root around my bag in search of a tissue to dab my tears. I was the mother, I tell him. To the best of my ability. I loved her more than anything in this world. She's a conundrum, I say. And Art looks at me with his soft, foreigner's eyes and says in his soft Hebrew, You did all you could, Yoella.

28.

After Meir's death, I quit the studio and take a job at the university's science library. I crave quiet and look forward to it.

On the sixth or seventh time I hand Art the books he has ordered, I accept his smile and smile back. I have been a widow almost six years and have known my daughter's whereabouts for some weeks. She's in Holland, in a city whose name I had never heard before—Groningen. I know she has two girls, and I have done the math: she conceived her eldest three or four months before flying in to tend to Meir in his final days, which means she already knew about her pregnancy then, and of all the things she kept hidden from me, this shames me to my core.

Art is very well-mannered, and in the smattering of words he offers when accepting the books, I detect an accent. When I ask, he replies that he was born and raised in Holland, and when I say, "My daughter lives in Holland, my granddaughters too," he gives a sympathetic nod. "And whereabout in Holland?" he asks. He has been living in Israel for forty-five years, but still selects his Hebrew words with the tentativeness of a foreigner.

"In Groningen," I spout out the answer, as if his question

was an easy one. I had granddaughters without being their grandmother, and until then had not told a single soul about it.

Only weeks later, after we dine at the restaurant across the street from his house, catch a play, and have sex will I admit that I have never met my granddaughters. That, aside from their birth dates, I know nothing about them. That I have not seen my daughter in six years. That I talk to her on occasion, but that is all she will allow. That she has never shared with me a single piece of information about her daughters, not even the fact of their existence. And even then, Art will remain unfazed. And by this I will know that with him by my side, there is nothing I can't weather.

As I have said before, I don't speak about Leah with anyone but Art. From time to time, running into people who knew her, who suddenly remember her, I have to find ways to catch them up without appearing sorrow-crazed or inspiring pity. I say everything with a smile, with breezy complaint. I say, this generation, everyone trying to find themselves. But she's happy, I insist. And that's all that matters.

Art is the sole recipient of the carefully culled details about my daughter and her family. Like me, he knows the names of my granddaughters. Their ages. Hobbies. The school they attend. I tell him about Leah's husband, Yohan, a drama teacher, and the bits and pieces I know about his life. But I don't show him even a single one of the photos of them I've found online, or say how many times a day I look at them.

On Leah, however, I turn up barely anything at all. She studied theater—her name appears in four student productions in the school where Yohan teaches—and seems to have dropped out during her second year. The student of staunch devotion. The standout. The Chosen One, who always caught the teacher's eye.

Shortly after moving in with him she became pregnant, and washed up on a less glamorous shore. Marriage record on the public database—Yohan posted online a photo with a few fellow teachers toasting the occasion—followed immediately by another pregnancy. She has a job, whose description I don't quite understand, at the local rec center, preschool coordinator, something like that, available for questions during office hours, every day 9:00 a.m. to 1:00 p.m., and on Tuesdays and Thursdays, 4:00 to 6:00 p.m. Every few weeks the photos are updated on the main website: the activities, the playground, the beautiful children engrossed in their games. I wait eagerly, anxiously, for the moment I find her in one of the photos. I scour the website day after day, morning and night, but she never reveals herself to me.

At the time, I told Meir everything about me; now I'm telling Art everything about Leah. What we were and how we were. He tells me a bit about his marriage to Talia, and about Sharona, the daughter they had together. Ever since Sharona's two children were born, the relationship between father and daughter has become closer; every few weeks Art visits them in Herzliya, and once a month he has them over for Friday night dinner.

"And you cook?"

"Of course." He prepares a stew his mother used to make in his childhood, *stamppot*. "It's basically a vegetable mash, and we often top it with smoked sausages."

Apparently it's a dish popular in the Netherlands, and Art's grandchildren, Israeli through and through, are crazy about it.

Little by little, Art also tells me about his parents, and their family trip to Israel when he was sixteen. His physicist father had planned a research year, and when that year came to a close, Art told his parents he was staying.

"I loved Jerusalem," he says. "I didn't want to go back."

"And they didn't try talking you out of staying?" I ask. "They just let you?"

He smiles. "Why wouldn't they?"

After twenty-eight years of marriage to one man, six of them posthumously, my knowledge about men has become obsolete. The penis once again poses a mystery. It seems that Art understands this, because when we have sex for the first time, he holds me in his arms for a long while, very slowly introducing me to his body before undressing me.

I n bed next to Art, I read about Lou Andreas-Salomé, the woman who so fascinated Rilke and Nietzsche. I read about how terribly worried Lou was for her father, while for her mother—

Listen to this, I tell Art.

Once during her earliest childhood she accompanied her mother to the seashore and watching her swim, cried out: "Darling, Mushka, please drown!"

Her mother replied with amazement, "But child, I would be quite dead then."

"Nitschewó!" roared Lou: "It makes no difference."

I read this to Art with feeling and flair, and we both burst into laughter.

29.

Now I thought that unhappy families no longer interested me, not one bit, I was interested only in the misery of happy families—the brittle middle. The family I grew up in, the family I built. I no longer concerned myself with the woman who grew up in abject poverty in Illinois and was driven off a train by a crying child, or with the French woman whose daughter spent two years in prison, or with the adopted woman from the terraced house in Lancashire and the absence of her early life. Leah and I had a beginning and continuum, but what explained us? How could I understand us?

She's a conundrum, I told Art. But so was I, a conundrum to my mother, and my mother to hers, and so on back through time to generation zero. And still, girls almost never abandoned their mothers, I told him. Not even the most horrible or meanest or most hard-hearted mothers—they remain their daughters, are their daughters always and forever, there's no undoing it. Why Leah? Throughout my life I've known only a handful of people who profess to have had a happy childhood; all the rest are survivors, everyone was given either too much or too little, life is always a long journey of healing from childhood. Why Leah?

30.

They sat together in the kitchen, talking and laughing.

"How much do you love your dad?" Meir asked, and Leah said, "A million kajillion."

"That's all?"

"Plus two."

"Now we're talking!"

And Leah snorted and said, "Ha ha, Dad. Hilarious."

They fell silent when I entered, as if I couldn't possibly understand.

But she, Leah, had asked me countless times over the years, "Do you love me, Mom?" and I would reply, "More than anything in the world," and she would ask, "You're sure?" and I would reply, "Plus seven," and she would say, "Round it up to ten and we'll shake on it," and never, not once, not in any way, shape, or form, did I return the question.

31.

Nearly a year goes by from the day Leah leaves until the boy calls, the man—I don't know how old this person with the deep and booming voice is, a voice rising from a well—and asks to speak to Leah's mother.

"Speaking," I say, heart racing. I have not seen my daughter in eleven months and have not heard from her in weeks.

The fellow informs me that Leah is in the mountains, in Nepal, that everything is fine, she's fine. He met up with her two weeks ago and she asked him to call us upon his return to Israel to let us know she's okay.

"In Nepal," I repeat his words. Forty-four days I have not heard from her. "In the mountains? She's in the mountains?"

"Yes," he says. And he says something else, about a phone that stopped working. Cell reception issues. I don't understand exactly what, and yet I rush to say, "Yes, of course."

"She'll be staying there a while longer," the fellow says. "A least a few more weeks. Maybe more."

I once knew a man with that kind of voice. I was working at an ad agency at the time, he was an account manager, and no matter what he said or wanted to say, his voice rippled and rattled through my body, the bass reverberating in all surrounding matter. And I thought back then, and still think now, that such a voice is a defect, a never-ending drama, with a voice like that, you can't say, she's fine, she'll be staying there a while longer, everything's fine.

So many things I want to say and ask. I sit down on the couch with the phone shaking in my hand. She turned nineteen two weeks ago, I called her countless times that day, the next day too. I didn't stop trying.

"Thank you for calling," I say, "thank you very much," and I hang up before his answer comes through.

At night, in bed, I tell Meir. A Yaniv called today, or Yariv, I couldn't recall his name, said Leah says hi. She's in the mountains, I tell Meir. In Nepal. There's no reception there. Or she doesn't have a phone. Never mind. It makes no difference.

Meir gives me a puzzled look. When did this happen? This morning? How could I not have told him until now? And before he can get another word out, I say, "She slept with him, that much is obvious. She's fine, sleeping around with men. Nothing to worry about."

Meir's look goes from surprise to shock. We've been out of our minds with worry, waiting on pins and needles, and finally we've been put at ease—what's wrong with me?

I cry and he hugs me. "Don't cry." All those years he has dreaded my tears, resented me for them. Now it's a load off. Until now we haven't talked about things as they are, and from here on, we will talk about them with increasing frequency, call them by their names and struggle to talk about anything else.

From that day on, they call regularly, every month or two. It's always men who crossed Leah's path, who trekked the mountains with her, the forests, the remote villages, places whose names are shot so quickly they land far outside my reach. Emissaries through which she sends word not to worry, everything's fine, she's fine. She asks that when they arrive at a main city, at an area with cell reception, in Israel, at home— they call us, and they do. Not to worry. She's fine. In these men's voices I hear complacent caution, that the world is theirs, that Leah is theirs, but now I'm ready for them. I never ask of them: Tell me. Tell me about Leah. I thank them. I say, thank you, thank you for calling. The moment I start to depend on them and their stories, I'll drown. And still I call her time after time, relentless. My calls go straight to voice mail.

Meir and I press forward. As the most senior employee, I can easily shovel my workload onto the other women in the studio, but I do the opposite; by virtue of that very seniority I take a chunk of their projects and use it to fill my every working hour, from the moment I arrive to the moment I exit the building, almost always after dark. At times, around midday, I leave the studio and head to one of the campus libraries, to sit there for an hour or two. They are imbued with the almost religious solemnity of bygone days, of churches. Or I tell my colleagues I have a headache, I have to go lie down, and I walk home, but instead of going up to the apartment, I get in the car and drive around for a while, head out of town and slip onto side roads I have become familiar with, an unpaved trail along a wadi, a dirt road at the foot of a mountain. Then I pull over to where no one can see, leave my phone on the seat, get out of the car, and start walking. I don't wait for anyone's call, don't wait for my daughter to call me. This is my only liberation.

At home, at night, I turn on all the lights—too many lights—except the one in Leah's room, whose door I have closed. I said to Meir, let's turn off the radiator in there, there's no point heating that room, it's a waste of money, we'll shut the door. Or maybe I said it's a waste of heat. And so our daughter's room remains hers, as if she is expected to return; our lives are the sum of these situations, what there is and what there isn't, we are the parents of a missing person, but the kind no one around us can understand, not even us; and in this darkness we fumble.

When Meir first tells me about the muscle pain plaguing him, I already know. I have been awakened more than once by the sound of suppressed groans. I accompany him to our GP, after which he's rushed to a series of scans. Results, consultations. Luck is not on our side. Without our knowing, the disease and Meir have been cohabitating for too long to split up.

Every time one of Leah's emissaries calls—always me, my phone—it takes me hours to get my thoughts straight, which can explain why I find it hard to say exactly when it dawns on me that it might all be a charade, that none of these men ever scaled up or down receptionless mountains with her, slept beside my daughter in forests, hiked with her to remote villages; that while they were on the phone with me, she was somewhere nearby, perhaps even right beside them, listening in, gesturing them to hurry up, and the next time they call I say, if you happen to run into her again, if you go back up the mountain, if you cross her path—you might just cross paths—tell her that her father is very sick.

She appears at the door less than a week later.

The three of us are together again, even if Meir is already not himself, neither in appearance nor in speech. He has drifted away from his essence, but is possibly more present than ever— it's hard to pin down the thing that happens to someone in his final days, whether he dwindles away or purifies.

Our nomad daughter is home. She is not sun-scorched. Nor are her calves muscular, or her hair an overgrown fern. She's not too thin—if anything, has put on weight—and her clothes, despite the multitude of colors and layers, are clean and kempt. I flash back to the summer between eleventh and twelfth grade, when she waited tables at the café in the local shopping mall. As if overnight, she learned to tuck her shirt into her skirt, chew bubble gum undetected, avoid leaning against the tables. She learned the proper way to pull her hair into a ponytail and not be too cozy with the customers.

"Mom."

She stood at the door. I reached out and touched her hair.

Affectionately, affectionately I used to ask her, when was the last time you washed your hair? It's due for a washing. Affectionately, I used to slide my hand over the heavy waterfall of her hair and say, we'll end up finding birds' nests in there, maybe a kitten, an antique Chinese coin.

"Liki?"

I burst into tears and embrace her, and she wraps her arms around me and says, "No, don't cry," and already it is hard to believe that she has been away for two years, that I have been in such agony. She is here. She is back.

I lead her into Meir's room. Our room. I worry that he'll become too excited, worry for his heart, but his face lights up with recognition and understanding, as if he has been expecting her, and in his new, drug-slurred voice, he says, "Leah'le."

Gingerly, she leans over him and his skeletal hands slowly climb up her back. Years ago, when he would come lunging through the door to bury his head in her stomach and growl and cackle, she would laugh so hard I feared she might choke. Now it's she who could choke him. She whispers something in his ear and they both laugh.

Meir dies in the hospital five days later. We both sit by him, holding his hands from either side of the bed. On the morning of his final day, the intuition of the doctors prompts them to tell us, stay. Don't go. Wait.

It's hard to find words for the moment it occurs; it is as otherworldly as it is prosaic. The plainness of the deceased's feet. And stacked up against this is the knowledge that we will no longer be able to ask him anything, not even the tiniest question, or offer an answer we have been putting off.

32.

Four times we went on vacation just the two of us, Leah and I. Stockholm, Copenhagen, Rome, Amsterdam. Six-year-old, eight-year-old, nine-year-old, eleven-year-old Leah. In those years Meir taught all through the summer or was busy with his books and essays and reluctant to travel, and I didn't object, I was glad. The three of us together was one thing, and when it was just Leah and me, we were another, we were different, I was different.

We slept in small hotels we had chosen from online booking sites, the trip started then, with its planning; we were manic about it, the pristine sheets that would await us on faraway beds, the towels perfumed with strange new scents, the tiny toiletries in the bathroom, the TV shows in foreign languages, these were all essential to the point. Foreign cities happen in their hotel rooms, the chilled crevices of the minibar, the questionably clean closets, the upholstered corridors; there was no point trying to explain this to Meir, whereas Leah needed no explanations. "The coffee at breakfast is catastrophic," I texted Meir from Rome, "but they have omelets to order, and the sweetest chef in the world cooks them as if his life depends on it." "The sea smells so good," Leah texted him from Copenhagen. "The water pressure in the shower is a dream and the towels are a miracle," I wrote him from Amsterdam. "If you were here you'd be spending the whole day showering-toweling." "The people on the street are so nice," Leah wrote him. "Everybody's so helpful with directions."

We had a marvelous time. The weightless European water glided over us in the shower, leaving our hair as feathery as after a fresh cut. The uncannily crisp sheets rearranged our sleep, which we floated into at night and slipped softly out of in the morning. I was drawn to the pleasant practicality of those rooms, which held nothing more than what was needed, were accommodating and easily cleaned; I was particularly drawn to their power to isolate time, to divide history into a beehive of histories, to preserve the most private existence and then wipe it clean, iron it out like the tightly tucked bedspread. With my daughter by my side it was all exhilarating and delightful, it was bliss; in the parallel universe of hotel rooms the values of our happiness shifted from relative to absolute.

We avoided subways, remained aboveground. We were captivated by the small parks, the lit shop windows. Copenhagen was luminous, even its sex shops were resplendent with light, vibrators and dildos in the vibrant pastels of toddler toys. Although we did once see, next to one of these shop windows, a very fat boy in doll-like neon sneakers, sobbing. On a tram in Amsterdam we saw a boy and girl who bore such a striking resemblance to each other they could have been twins, passionately kissing. In a café whose chairs spilled out onto the curb we saw an older woman treating herself to a slice of cream pie:

leaning carefully over her teacup and pie, she polished it off with poise and exactitude. In Rome we sat in a pizzeria next to an American family trading dad jokes: "What do you call a hippie's wife? Mississippi!" "What did the plate say to the cup? Dinner's on me!" A cute family, quick to laugh, a hulking mother and father in chinos and tentlike Hawaiian shirts, and their three daughters, slender Asian girls in summer dresses. We weren't the only ones staring, the whole restaurant couldn't take their eyes off them. I knew a girl whose adoptive parents went to great lengths to blur the seams so she would blend perfectly into her new family—the disturbing drama of discovery awaiting on the horizon, a discreet hair trigger. But when Caucasian parents adopt Asian girls, it's an adventure open to the public. The mother spoke to her girls with the slow intonation often used with children, speech ensnared in the echoing loops of self-consciousness. She was relying on what she had read and learned, and seemed to have no idea how fluid life was, and how one could be right and wrong at the same time, by which I mean to say, she loved her daughters and loved being their mother, that much was clear, and yet everyone was staring. Such a sinuous road. We finished our meal and were about to head back to the hotel when a man walked in with a leashed dog, pocketed a few sachets of sugar from the counter, and asked the waiter for a glass of hot water. The waiter asked him to leave. We saw many of his kind in Rome, handsome men who had drifted too far on life's current and fed their dogs anything they could get their hands on. We picked up and left and didn't exchange a single word the whole way back to the hotel, only held hands—we knew what we had seen.

When it was just the two of us, Leah and me, we reflected each other in purest form. No one intervened or interfered, and even if I was angry at her for a moment or two, or if one of us picked a fight, we immediately reconciled. She could not bear even the slightest tension between us, and that is what I held on to. We rented bicycles and rode to the park, strolled hand in hand and bought things, knickknacks of all sorts—hairpins, pens, dolls. In Rome, at lunch, I let her have a sip of my cocktail and then had another two myself, and we talked nonstop and roared with laughter, people turning to stare. We ate exactly what and as much as we wanted, and in the evening, nine at the latest, wherever we traveled, we were already tucked in our hotel room—shower, TV, herbal tea, curling up in bed, chatting, head over heels, bleary-eyed with love.

On that trip to Amsterdam, we stayed in a hotel overlooking the side of the Anne Frank House. We couldn't see the entrance to the building, only the long line that wrapped around it at nearly all hours of the day, a snaking line that rattled with wrappers and bags and maps and hushed talk; no matter how hot, nothing could get the crowd to surrender their place and retreat into the awninged havens of the nearby cafés and shops; they were waiting there every morning when we left the hotel and every afternoon when we returned to our room. On our fourth day in the city we joined the line and stood for hours alongside everyone else—Leah insisted. At eleven years old she maneuvered quickly between sentimentality and sarcasm, yielding herself to pop ballads about love and loneliness while forever on the lookout for any display of overearnestness, especially from Meir and me, especially from me, before being once again swept up in the emotional tumult of teenage girls—trivial matters ultimately, banal. She read the stories of Helen Keller and Sarah Aaronsohn, tribulations that touched her heart. She read Anne Frank's diary and made me read it right after she was done. She wanted to talk about Anne for hours on end. She thought she and Anne could have been wonderful friends, that she herself could have been a wonderful Anne; that had they been sisters, they would have written a diary together. She wanted to see the room in the attic, found the notion electrifying, to be walking around Anne's room (walls remember everything), and was stunned to see—from my strained expression and impossibly soft voice—how these very things annoyed me. The muted Holocaust experience this room supplied its visitors, its distance from the camps, its aesthetics, the winding line day in, day out, year after year, to peek into the room that housed a little girl during the Holocaust, an over-the-top, runaway metaphor for suffering.

We argued. She argued with me and wouldn't let me agree with her if it was disingenuous. But hours of walking and standing in the snake-line had exhausted me, my feet ached, I wanted to return to the hotel. "And besides," she said, "as annoying as this line is, it's also powerful. You're not alone when you come here, you know? It's been so many years and people keep coming, from all over the world, even people who aren't Jewish, everyone's heard about Anne and come to visit her."

"You're right," I said.

"Stop it," she huffed, "I'm being serious."

"I know," I replied, "you're right, the line does add to the experience."

It only upset her more. The quick concessions made to avert confrontation.

When we finally got in, she was withdrawn, shaken without sharing; I was familiar with that form of punishment, I hugged her. "Anne Frank would have been very pleased if she knew how many people were walking around her house right now," I said. We made up; she didn't know how to fight with me and struggled with it. That night, after we turned off the TV and bedside lamps and curled up in the bleached hotel sheets, her face against the pillow suddenly seemed so young, her voice still too high-pitched and dulcet to say things as she wished them to be said.

"Thanks for waiting with me today," she said. "I know you were tired."

I leaned in and kissed her forehead. "But it's odd," I said, "because while reading Anne Frank's diary you already know how it ends."

She considered me with sleep tugging at her eyelids. "So?"

"Think about it," I said. "The readers know the ending but she, Anne, didn't. It makes for a strange read, when the reader knows more than the author."

She thought about it for a moment. We both did. And she, my daughter, with the same conscientiousness she carried with her everywhere, even when she was beat, said, "Yes, that's true. Life is like that for everyone. We read our story without knowing how it'll end."

"My baby," I said, "my smart baby."

"My mom," she said, "what are we going to do with you?"

That night she was out like a light but I stayed up, swelling with a sense of urgency, waiting for her to wake up so I could tell her what I had avoided telling her that whole day—that Anne Frank's was not only a story of attempted rescue, it was also one of betrayal, and that's what riled me in the romanticized drama of the line, in the mass pilgrimage up the attic stairs, the falling in love with the hiding Anne, the Anne surviving from one day to the next, the fragile glazing of salvation. I was unable to sleep, was suspended just inches above it, dangling. I felt very bad. Very bad. It occurred to me that if I were a hotel housekeeper opening the doors to the rooms in the morning, I would wait before entering. People leave behind things that are invisible but urgent; I would wait for the rooms to rid themselves of these remnants before stepping in. I don't know when I finally fell asleep. The flight home was scheduled for the following day and I didn't want to go back.

33.

Five weeks after Meir's death I drove Leah to the airport. I knew exactly what I was going to say, already had the words lined up in my head. Forty minutes in the car with no escape hatch. Our rides to the airport used to be the kickoff to an adventure waiting to unfold, and it felt the same now. Leah got in the car, placed her coat on her lap and her hands over the coat. I turned on the radio. After a few moments she reached out to turn it down, then lowered her hand to her side. I waited a while before cranking it back up and only much later, when we stopped at the airport terminal, did I put my hand on hers. It wasn't too late. I pulled into the drop-off zone and we got out of the car. I knew that I was going to talk, that I couldn't not talk. I heaved her giant duffel bag out of the trunk. A car came up behind ours, waiting for us to clear the lane, and I rushed back into the driver's seat. "Come here," I called out to her from behind the wheel, and she bent over the open passenger window and poked her head in. I leaned across the seat, cupped her face with both my hands, and kissed her on the mouth like we used to. The curt honk sounding behind us quickly broke us apart. I could see her in the side mirror, standing there, watching as I drove away.

34.

It happened to me before, wanting a man who sat next to me on the train for the heat his body radiated or the sound of his voice as he spoke on the phone, or if he stood in front of me in line at the supermarket and placed a plain loaf of bread, a bottle of wine, and cheese on the conveyor belt. Meir gathered his groceries and put them in a tote bag with large, flat hands. They looked dry and warm, I knew how they would smell when he cradled my face and I wanted that. I inched closer, inhaled the faint scent of wool and fabric softener, almost touched him. The wine and cheese and silvering temples gave off a laid-back maturity, self-awareness and economic calm, and I wanted him then and there, but he didn't look behind him even once, tucked his wallet back in his pocket, took his tote, and left. I had to wait until I saw him again.

For twenty-two years we lived together, and after he died and Leah took off again, going back to work was a struggle.

After a day at the studio I holed away at home. I was always careful when it came to neighborly relations, particularly wary of overly friendly neighbors, the kind whose neighborliness was imposed on me at every staircase run-in. I once read about an elderly couple whose dream it was to decamp from the city and buy a secluded house where they could live in peace and quiet, and how happy they were after the move—until they discovered that their new neighbor from the only other house in the whole area was determined to pay them daily visits.

Most days I hurried home from the studio. I was sapped by humans, yet still wanted to see people, wanted to see but not hear them, become a little deaf to them, like my mother had, and that was why, when I caught wind of the impending retirement of the university's science librarian, I applied for the position. I was relieved. The library was strict about preserving the quiet, and if it was broken, it was in whispers.

35.

I loved Meir for many years, and would have stayed with him had he not died. I would not have left. I knew what to remember and remembered everything about our falling in love and who wanted what, and if there were discrepancies in our recollections, I didn't back down.

I didn't see him again at the supermarket. It was in the university cafeteria; spotting his back as he stood at the checkout counter, I quickly sat myself down at one of the tables. Few sat there. Most customers, upon being handed their paper bags, scurried off. I waited for him to receive his order and walk away; I thought that I would keep my eyes on my newspaper, and he would disappear. Meir swept his gaze across the cafeteria and took a seat at a nearby table. We exchanged smiles. I couldn't remain there without continually glancing his way, so I got up and left. When he showed up at the studio a few weeks later I was bewildered, as if he had heard the distant drumming of my heart and tracked it down.

I looked at his order sheet. "Professor Driman?"

Every so often a professor would walk into the studio with revisions to the work they had commissioned, and then we could put a face to the name on the order, and they, in turn, would make a show of asking for our names; we were a testament to their attractiveness, we were the studio women, embedded in the background layer of academic life, sitting over our light-boxes lit up from below like spaceships and listening attentively when spoken to.

Meir Driman projected utter calm. Not shyness, but a sense of being given to himself. He was sixteen years my senior, and I instantly wanted to sleep with him, to wake up in his book-brimming apartment, which I could imagine to the last detail: sheets in an outdated pattern, terrazzo tiles, those rheumatic Jerusalem radiators. Two years had passed since I'd locked myself at home for long weeks, unable to bring myself to step outside; the bat whose wings had cast their shadow on me in my youth had swooped down to land directly on my heart, and even when I managed to heave myself out of bed, I couldn't shower, get dressed, brush my hair, eat. I parted ways with the ad agency I worked at and stayed put at home. Two of my friends knew what was going on and paid daily visits, sometimes twice a day, bringing groceries (I barely ate; sometimes only a yogurt or a couple of cookies at night), taking out the garbage. The meds eventually helped, pressed the felt dampers against the strings. When I recovered I slept a few times with someone I knew from high school, a motorcycle repairman who expected and asked nothing of me and was always generous with his liquor stash. And then with an account manager from the ad agency, who called to inquire in his baritone voice where I had disappeared to. I slept with my upstairs neighbor, a physics student, when he came to tell me that he was moving out. I started working at the university's graphic design studio, where I was allotted the corner light table farthest from the door, and with earbuds in I could hardly hear the music that was always playing from an old cassette player.

Meir called the evening of the day he'd appeared at the studio. If I hadn't been interested in him, it would have made for an awkward situation for both of us, but I was interested, very much so, and when we met up I immediately wanted him to know everything about me. I told him about my father's passing when I was fourteen, the dragged-out years of adolescence, the months of depression, the meds. I told him things that as a girl or teenager I would never have revealed, but that as an adult I underscored—they became the crux of my stories. I felt good. Hadn't felt so good in years. We talked about children. I told Meir, when I have a daughter she'll know how to say yes, that's not a problem. I'm not worried about that. My worry is that she won't know how to say no. That has to be taught to girls, I said, and I'll teach her. And Meir said, it's different nowadays, it's a different world, your daughter will grow up in a new world that neither you nor I can even imagine. And I nodded and said, nevertheless, nevertheless, how carelessly girls are cornered into being women—and I emphasized *women*—that will never change.

We had Leah. She was one of those girls who was endlessly loved by their parents and just a little less loved by the rest of the world; and there came a time when I sensed she resented that. The disparity. Maybe she didn't find herself pretty. But to her father and me she was the most beautiful girl in the world, and the love of our lives.

36.

I understood who Meir was, I did. There was a brief marriage in his past which he told me about offhandedly. A sab-
batical at the Sorbonne, a young woman named Dorit, the
daughter of Israelis who emigrated to France when she was six,
a modest ceremony at city hall attended by a few of the bride's
Parisian friends (who called her Doreen), the effort to wedge
himself into a normal life at forty. They planned to divide their
time between the two countries. Five months into the marriage, it took only a few mornings of filling out forms to untie
the knot. Meir returned to Israel. Over the following two years,
there were other women, and at forty-three he was smitten
with one of his PhD students, who became pregnant. Michaela.
He mentioned her from time to time over the course of our
years together. The pregnancy ended on its own a short while
later, he said, and I could tell from his voice that this was ultimately a story of narrow escape.

Until she was born, Meir could have lived his life without
Leah. He did not want children, everything he saw around
him left him unconvinced of their necessity. He did not notice them, neither on the street nor in photos nor at friends'

houses—children did not capture his attention. He worked tirelessly every day, taught graduate students, supervised doctoral students, sank into his research for months and years and was dedicated to his life just the way it was. But when Leah was born, he instantly fell in love with her, and loved her with every fiber of his being; and when she left us at eighteen and did not come back, he faded into illness.

He was forty-six the summer I saw him at the supermarket, and a few weeks later he showed up at the studio, after which we never parted. But there were times when I left the house in tears, got into my car, started the engine, and drove around town for thirty minutes, an hour, two, until he called and, with soft words, steered me back.

When he was already very sick, Meir suffered terribly from the cold. But with the windows closed from morning to night the room was stifling, so in the early evening I would cover him with three blankets, open the windows, and lie beside him in the dark. We would talk for a bit. He was tired and weak and so was I. And still, one night he said, "I thought that after you gave birth, I would have to have you committed."

I listened breathlessly. The months of pregnancy with Leah were a horror ripening from within—the thing that was growing inside me, forming from my flesh, was also entirely sealed off and subjugating.

"I saw how you were holding on," Meir continued. "I knew you were holding on by your fingertips. I remember thinking, she'll have the baby and then fall to pieces. She'll never be able to take care of anyone, ever. I thought that after the birth I'd have to raise the baby on my own and also take care of you."

It hurt that he would say this. The words he chose.

"You were off your rocker," he said. "But then Leah was born and a miracle happened. She was born—and you came back. Just like that, you were your old self again. You loved her so much and took care of her, everything seemed so simple. I couldn't believe it. It was months before I could believe."

By the beat of his breathing, I knew he was in pain. I eased him onto his side to relieve the pressure, and he closed his eyes and fell asleep. I left, coming back an hour later to close the windows.

37.

L eah's first crushes are free falls. She drops her love on children's heads; her love is momentum and mass and there's nothing to slow down the drama, or rather, there is no drama; hers alone, and in her control, her crushes are exempt from uncertainty. Love as a decision, devoid of plot or mischief, dependent on no one and nothing.

In preschool she is in love with Yair for three years straight; in first, second, and half of third grade she is in love with Hagai. The following year a new student, Avri, joins the class, and Leah falls for him unreservedly.

"He's athletic," she tells me with a twinkle in her eye, and as it turns out, Avri often passes her the ball during dodgeball. "He's cute," she says, "a real cutie-pie." At school she asks him if he wants to be her boyfriend and he says yes, but a few days later he passes her a note in class that reads "We have to break up."

She promptly writes back: "Why?" and when the answer arrives, she passes him a doodle of a flower and two words, "No worries."

All this she tells me upon her return from school, and I sit down beside her. Should I hug her? What should I say? I run my hand over her hair.

"And then he wrote that he's confused."

"Confused?"

"Confused and tired."

"Confused and tired? He wrote that he's confused and tired?"

"He wrote 'confused and tyerd.' He makes spelling mistakes. But I can help him."

"Leah . . ."

She shrugs. "Whatever, I don't care. I love him and want to be his girlfriend."

It goes on. When Avri brushes off her attempts to speak to him, she's saddened but not irate or indignant. Is this admirable or alarming? Heartwarming or heartrending? In my daughter's world, there is no give and take in love, nothing is tallied, there is no reward and no restraint. Meir also tries his best, with calm conversation, soft speech, not to stop her, not to crush her loving, free-flowing nature but to slightly temper it.

"It's okay, Dad," she reassures him. "Don't worry."

Avri's family moves away over summer break, and the following year, for many months, Leah is quieter than usual. She excels in all her classes. She's fascinated by the stories of the Bible, and I, who could never relate to them as such, find myself mesmerized hearing them from her. Days go by. Avri is forgotten.

But shortly before Passover she returns home altered, a little girl again, a munchkin, raving about the story of the binding of Isaac. It seems at first that the story has been defused—the Bible teacher acting as a buffer, padding it with words about the power of faith and devotion—and yet, to ensure that whatever has eluded her is indeed nameless and abstract, Leah recounts the story from start to finish. She unshoulders it and drops it at my feet with a thud.

"It's an amazing story," she says.

"It certainly amazes me," I say.

She considers me. The story is amazing, but in what way exactly?

"Abraham amazes me," I say.

She can't hold back. "God put him in an impossible position," she bursts out. Words entrusted to her by her teacher, which must be, and are, relayed. "He was faced with an impossible dilemma," she insists.

"Dilemma?" My voice rings too high. "There's no dilemma here."

"No, no, no. He lived in different times, Mom. Back then, people thought the sea was God, the wind was God, the sun, the sky, the stars—all of it, God. They didn't know. They believed and they were afraid."

"And that's supposed to matter?" I ask her, and wish I hadn't. I go on. "It doesn't matter. There's only one possible answer to God's request of Abraham: Never. You will never get my child. Not in a million years, not if you kill me here and now, not if you set the whole world on fire. I would tell God, do your worst. My child, from me, you won't get. Not from me."

Leah's eyes well up.

"Not from my hands," I say, as if it is beyond guessing, as if I'm better than everyone else. "Never."

"And you know what?" Leah says. "God would have clapped."

"If there was a God and if he had hands," I say.

She laughs. "He would have clapped!"

I feel that I have deserted her, that I failed to share the burden, that with my certitude I put her on one side with Abraham while I stood on the other.

38.

The night before her first day of middle school, Leah struggles to fall asleep. There is a whole to-do about her outfit leading up to it. She picks out a skirt I don't care for, and when I say, "But that's just me, go with whatever you like, whatever you think looks nice," it's already too late. Sobs and sobs. She shuts herself in her room for long moments before coming out in a pair of black jeans and a black T-shirt. She stands in front of me, waiting. I tell her she's beautiful. Absolutely perfect. And she hangs a hug on me. "I'm sorry I'm like this," she says. "I'm just excited, it'll pass."

But that entire year she dissects her body's imperfections. The slight discoloration above her eyelid. Enlarged pores on her chin. The curve of her nose. They overtake her reflection in the mirror as she disapprovingly outlines each one.

"It's a lost cause," I say. "Never mind your birthmark and your pores, but your nose? I don't see a solution to that."

"Mom, come on."

"I'm serious. Should I start looking into convents?"

"You're not taking this seriously and it's annoying."

"Well, fortunately, you won't have to see that much of me when you're in the convent."

"Quit it!"

"Me quit it? Me?"

"Yes."

"Gorgeous and dumb."

"You're such a pain."

But her hug is grateful.

That year, there was a scrawny and sullen British singer she listened to for hours on her headphones and stalked on the internet, poring over photos of him with a revolving cast of girlfriends. She deemed them all beautiful, perfect, worthy of all forms of love. And there was another one, a scrawny and sullen TV game show host she used to call "the divine," and when he married his girlfriend to great media fanfare, Leah decided to copy her haircut—a long French bob with bangs, which to my relief we both still liked the morning after. From time to time, when she saw young couples nuzzling on the street, or even just walking their dog, her eyes would mist over, lashes fluttering. "Oh, that's exactly what I want, Mom. That." And it was a game but it was also the truth, her heart pounding on her open palm. "It's so sweet, Mom. Look, is there anything sweeter? There just isn't. I want a boyfriend. Will I have one? We'll kiss and walk his dog and sit on the beanbags in my room and laugh about stuff. Do you think I'll ever be like that with a boy? That we'll sit and laugh about stuff? Don't worry, we won't have sex. Only later. I want a boyfriend and a dog. And a car. And a driver's license. Will it happen? I have it all planned out."

I loved looking at her hands, those delicate fingers that were always so cold I'd have to rub them warm, those slender arms she now covered with blue-inked reminders and doodles of eyes and lips and lips and eyes (stop drawing on yourself, I'd tell her, use paper, use notepads, I'll buy you whatever you need, don't draw on yourself), the svelte body that suddenly swayed to a beat playing in her head and swelling up inside her—poetry in motion that framed her youth and played tricks on me.

"I have it all planned out," she told me. "Listen."

She had it all planned out, which classmates she'd agree to have as boyfriends and which she'd reject (there were two boys, she decided, whom she especially fancied).

She worked out where they would go together, what they would do, and the topics they would talk about.

She mapped out the moment they would kiss.

These imaginings of hers were cutouts from TV shows, and she shared every detail with me. I'm not exaggerating. She told me everything.

How their hands would find each other in the popcorn tub in the darkened movie theater.

How they would drink hot cocoa in a café on a cold day (exterior view: fogged-up café windows).

How they would stretch out on the carpet in her bedroom ("Wait! Serious problem! I don't have a carpet. I have to get a carpet!") or in his room, and read each other funny quotes they'd found online, and make pizza together (floury foreheads and noses).

She planned out the Scrabble matches, the dog walks in the

pouring rain, rushing home for hot tea and cookies. The dog was crucial. Indispensable.

She was innocent and sweet and offered herself up to the world unconditionally.

"You're such a nut," I'd say, wrapping my arms around her. "You little intimacy freak. Your boyfriend is going to be one lucky boy. The luckiest of all lucky boys."

39.

In eighth grade they suddenly remember. The school sends out a pamphlet advertising a series of lectures for parents, *Practical Advice on Healthy Adolescent Sexual Behavior*; *Sex and Sexuality: How to Talk to Your Teenager*; *Sex, Sexuality, and the World Wide Web*. The lecturers are all academics; it's a strict policy in that school, I've noticed this over the years, they're scared of spiritual counselors, are swayed only by science. But I had already seen to it. A year earlier I'd made sure Leah knew everything that could be of use to her, sat her in front of a Norwegian sex-ed show for teenagers that I'd found online, short videos with English subtitles, a show that addressed things unapologetically. Their approach appealed to me. They showed a cock up close. They explained how and when hair sprouts around it and the testicles fill. They explained how the penis functions, the mechanics of the blood vessels that enable it to become erect. They explained nocturnal emissions. In the episode about the female adolescent body, they lingered over the breasts, the various patterns that body hair would imprint on them, the female orifices. I sat beside her and translated the subtitles when there was a word she didn't understand. Watch, I told her, we'll watch it together, and if you have more questions afterward, ask. It's okay if you're embarrassed, I told her, I'm a little embarrassed too, but it's all true, it's literally the facts of life, and it's important to know.

"The facts of life?" she asked.

"Yes."

"Literally?"

"Yes, Leah Driman, literally."

"Okay, I was just making sure."

I couldn't bear it any other way. I was petrified by the randomness by which she might see a cock for the first time. In online porn. Or the filthy hand of a public masturbator. Or the pervert on the bus who'd rub up against her from behind, causing her to turn around and look down, and for a moment even to think she should apologize. My mind cooked up even worse scenarios, the entire history of female shame and its calamities. No. Not going to happen. I wouldn't have it.

She giggled at the screen and gasped, "Oh my God," "Oh mercy," "Help!" And I laughed too. About the penis close-up she said, "TMI. TMI." About the vagina close-up she said, "Gruesome."

I said, "Liki, the vagina is the passageway to all creation, it's nature in all its glory," and she shrugged and said, "Ah ha. I don't think so. It doesn't . . . doesn't look very glorious. I'm sorry." We laughed again. She was happy. She was twelve years old and suddenly enlightened. I had vivid adolescent memories of the darkness shrouding sex, there was no benefit to it, I was happy we had cast a light into that corner.

I attended the lectures organized by the school the following year, just to be on the safe side. In the last of the series, I sat in the auditorium a row behind Arza's mother, who kept edging up her bun dexterously, offhandedly, cross-legged in delicate gold sandals, taking notes on the slides projected onto the large screen. Outlines. Reminders on the subjects we were to broach at home urgently. The lecturer had us scared out of our wits—it turned out the internet was steadily encroaching on every aspect of our children's lives, that everything we had neglected for so long was possibly beyond repair. That we might have woken up far too late. I looked around. Other parents were jotting away. I took a piece of paper and a pen out of my bag but didn't write. I doodled, no longer listening.

40.

I hear about Dennis on Leah's very first day of high school. He's one of the kids my daughter doesn't know from middle school, but Arza, who sang with him in the choir, knows him and isn't impressed. "Arza says he's a scatterbrain," Leah says. "And he didn't talk to anyone the whole day. Not a single word! And at recess he took out a notebook and started drawing. A total weirdo."

In his Facebook profile photo I see a boy with wavy fair hair, a gorgeous creature with a wistful, faraway look, and when Leah asks, "Well? Well? Well?" I say the photo is too small to really see anything—leaving wiggle room for whatever will come. In the future, if need be, I'll be impressed. But Leah rests her hand on the photo and then on her heart: "I'm in love."

With the requisite grin, I say, "For a brilliant girl, you can be pretty dumb sometimes," and she plops herself on the couch in a fainting gesture.

I let her be. Over the following weeks I'm a sympathetic audience to her performance of a girl in love. I try to be home when she comes back from school to launch into her stories, which now invariably involve Dennis—her eyes skyward, dramatic landing on the kitchen chair—"He's so cute, Mom. You cannot believe the cuteness." And then she imitates the way he runs his hand through his hair while he thinks, and that thing he does with his lower lip, the slight tugging. "I'm crazy crushing," she says, "crazy."

At night, in bed, I tell Meir, she's taking it too far, she's too much, and Meir says, it's nothing, she's just trying it on for size, you know your daughter, she's in love with falling in love. But at the first parent-teacher conference of the year he joins me, paying close attention during the round of introductions. Dennis's parents are a handsome but somber couple, older than the other parents. So fair-skinned. And not from here. Russians. The mother glances at her phone every few moments, and toward the end of the meeting the father takes a call, apologizes, and steps outside.

"Good genes," Meir teases on our way home. "As far as I'm concerned we can put a down payment on a wedding hall."

"Funny," I say, "absolutely hilarious."

"I always wanted a sexy mother-in-law."

"Oh, can it."

S uddenly the holidays are behind us and the year is in full swing. The daylight hours grow shorter and the school day longer. Leah comes home at five, sometimes six. Twice a week she goes to the swimming pool straight after school and comes home at eight, having already showered, her hair damp and her eyes a little red. When I reach for her frozen cheeks and ask that she at least wear a hat on her way home, she dismisses me with a smile. "It's all good, Mom. I'm starving. Focus on that."

On those days I have no reason to rush home from work, and every so often I make a detour to Meir's office. Years ago, when we were fucking on the old couch there, late at night, when we thought the building was empty and didn't really care if it wasn't, one of the cleaning ladies opened the door, gave a start, and fled. Today I make us tea in the kitchenette and split a pastry that I'd picked up on the way over. In recent years we have reduced our carbs, limiting our pastry intake to at most a weekly indulgence. "Let them eat cake," I say as I serve him his half, and he smiles. But after we have our tea and talk for a while, I know I ought to get going, I can feel him getting restless.

Alone at home I wait anxiously for Leah and Meir to return, as if when they walk through the door I might be found out, for doing what, I don't know. I'm afraid of falling asleep on the couch, of them finding me asleep, so I remain on my feet, tidying up, washing dishes, cleaning, arranging the closets. A scenario I have invented like a game grips my thoughts. I miss the early days of motherhood and seek them out.

T ry, Dr. Schonfeler suggests. Just start, with plain words. He's asking me to tell him about the meaningful human relationships in my life right now—meaningful relationships in my life have always interested him. In the past, I sometimes found his calm and caring tone grating, was embarrassed by the therapeutic ring to it, whereas now I have no problem sharing. "I was afraid I wouldn't love my child," I say, "that I might see myself in her all the time."

This clearly doesn't satisfy Dr. Schonfeler. He wants to get to the core of the dread, the root of its cause. I open my mouth to elaborate but he stops me.

"Were you afraid of the irreversibility of it?" he asks.

I'm not sure I'm following.

"A child is born," Dr. Schonfeler says, "and there's no turning back. You can't undo a child, it's for life."

"Oh," I gulp, "no, no. It's the other way around. I was afraid of the reversibility. It's the reversibility that scared me."

We talk for a while. Dr. Schonfeler is of the impression that I've learned to talk about my problems openly. Sixteen years have gone by since I first sat across from him, it's hard to remember who we were, time replaces us, and still, whenever I've seen him since then, I've felt a trust for him as if he knew me. That first time, a friend gave me a ride over and waited for me out in the car to drive me back. I was afraid of leaving my house, afraid of getting into the car, afraid of getting out, afraid of entering the clinic. After I walked in, I sank into the armchair in his office and held my breath as if underwater. Dr. Schonfeler always kept the lights dimmed and his voice low. He asked a few questions and recommended starting me on two types of meds right away, one for immediate relief and the other for the long haul. He told me to hang in there, I remember that vividly. He said, hang in there today and tomorrow. And then hang in there one more day. And then another. And by next week it'll already be better. He wasn't particularly interested in the circumstances that got me where I was. The nucleus story is always the same, he said, the plot is secondary. And yet I told him, because I felt the story was of the utmost importance: an affair with one of my military commanders, which began shortly after my enlistment and spanned eight years. Married, father of three, you know you're my everything. Then a year of repeated breakups. A nervous breakdown. Forty-four pounds shed in four months, and three weeks without a single foray out of the house. Dr. Schonfeler said, "For the moment there's no point in much talking, let's get you stabilized first." He shifted in his chair, ill at ease. It felt as if only a few minutes had passed since I'd walked in, when in fact it had been over an hour.

My friend drove me home after my appointment, sat next to me, and watched as I ate an apple. Painstakingly. Overcoming the strenuous effort of swallowing. A week later I felt better, and two weeks after that I arrived at Dr. Schonfeler's clinic by taxi. I was grateful to my friend for her help all those weeks, but I no longer desired her presence, and downright scorned her visits. There was another friend who had visited me on occasion during that difficult period, and I turned her away too. A new chapter, I believe that was what I had in mind. I slept with a few men, was eager to go out and dive back into my life. I started working at the graphic design studio. I met with my mother for the first time in three months and apologized for my long absence. I'm sorry, I said, I was busy at work, I didn't have time to breathe.

When Dr. Schonfeler asks about meaningful relationships in my life, he's asking who I talk to, who I tell things to. I want another girl, I say. Leah's thirteen, I'm forty-three, I want another girl but realize it could be a boy. I'm okay with that. I did the tests, I'm still fertile. Actually, I say, I came so you would tell me whether another pregnancy could bring on another psychological crisis. My pregnancy with Leah dragged me down to a low worse than all the other lows that preceded it, such that now, almost fourteen years later, I'm still petrified. But I'm also ready for it, I tell him. I just want to be prepared. I mean, what will happen to Leah? If I get pregnant and have another breakdown, what will become of Leah? How much could she handle?

"And what about Meir?" Dr. Schonfeler asks.

"Meir?"

"What does Meir think about taking this step?"

I say, "I haven't talked to Meir yet. I wanted to talk to you first."

"And are you going to talk to him?" Dr. Schonfeler asks. Life replaces us, as I have mentioned, but Dr. Schonfeler still knows me better than anyone.

"Of course," I say. "That goes without saying."

A while later I go off the pill. When I inform Meir about a late period and the results of a home pregnancy test, I see in his eyes all I need to know. I wait only a day before scheduling an appointment at a private clinic for the following week. The place is spotless and the doctor affable. The evening after the abortion, I lock myself in the bathroom. To simulate crying, I pinch my cheeks and slap them with wet hands. I flush the toilet, wait a minute, and flush again. When I step out, Meir immediately asks what happened, and I tell him. I know exactly what to say, I did my research. Heavy bleeding, I say, sharp cramps in the afternoon, and now this. We're not going to have another baby, I say, and he holds me in a long embrace.

There was an earlier incident, I remember, the start of the beginning. I was nine, maybe ten, I was sitting in the classroom and trembling, something had gone wrong, and all of a sudden I was at the nurse's office and my father was on his way to pick me up. At home my mother was waiting for us, and someone had arrived, a doctor. But he wanted only to talk, ask questions. Then I was absent from school, I don't remember exactly for how long. My teacher called regularly, every day or two, and spoke with my mother. I started taking medication that my mother referred to as tablets. She didn't ignore things, she called them by names that suited her. Every morning, in a saucer on the kitchen counter, my tablets were waiting for me. I don't remember when or how it was decided that I would stop taking them, but I did. I returned to being a regular child and posed no more problems. Every so often I'd wake up drenched in an emotion that was neither dread nor guilt, an inkblot dispersing in water, but it lasted less than an hour. Perhaps I failed to understand the significance of my childhood, or understood it and made a point to take with me only what I could use, because the fact is I forgot all about it for years, maybe until this moment.

41.

My neighbor Ora knocked on the door. She'd been away for two weeks, on an organized tour to Europe, suddenly I didn't remember just where. France, Holland, maybe Belgium. She looked fabulous, radiant in her new haircut. She said, make me coffee, you won't believe the story I have for you.

I didn't like it when she fizzed like that. Talked too loud. But I wanted to hear. We had become closer since Meir's death. It wasn't a friendship, I kept away from those. By then I had already cut off most of my ties, didn't want to tell anyone about Leah, that she was avoiding me, that in recent years I called her only when I could endure the coldness of her voice. It embarrassed me. I didn't want to be confronted with questions and have to explain, but sitting with Ora now I was happy she had come.

It was a marvelous trip, Ora said. A good group, everyone always on time, except for one, a widower, not that old. Raphael. Rafi. So annoying. And on the bus he always insisted on sitting by the window, said he had motion sickness. And the tour guide was excellent. Although he did an awful lot of explaining, they always explain too much, how much information can a person take in? But a nice guy, from Haifa. Went to the Technion. And the thing that happened happened in Groningen—a nice city, she said, quaint, all of Holland is. After a visit to the maritime museum, they'd dispersed for thirty minutes of free time to explore the town before reconvening back at the bus, everyone but Rafi, again. Waiting for Rafi. Story of our lives. And she, Ora, took her seat on the bus and looked out the window. Two cute girls were sitting by a fountain, and she thought to herself, what adorable girls, where's their mother? And then she saw the mother on a bench nearby, keeping an eye on them.

"I looked at her," Ora said, "squinted. I couldn't believe it."

My grip on my coffee mug tightened. Over the past months I'd spoken with Leah only once. She was in Thailand, she said, working on a small organic farm. Mostly cooking, sometimes cleaning. I didn't ask questions, I let her speak, didn't want to poke holes in her story. Now I tried to draw the mug to my lips, but my hands trembled. Ora didn't have children. She didn't have a driver's license. She didn't share her life with anyone, never had. These avoidances were all related, rooted in the same dysfunction.

"I thought I was going nuts," Ora continued. "I looked at her. Leah? Yoella's Leah? What is she doing here? Can't be. Is that Leah?! She looks just like her, her doppelganger! I got up, told the driver, wait for me, I'll be back in a sec; I got off the bus and started walking toward them, I don't know why, what I was thinking to myself. I was thinking, maybe I'll take a photo of her for Yoella. Yoella has got to see this, she's got to!"

Ora paused for a moment, ran out of breath, dizzy with

excitement. I had always felt sorry for her, thought it was easy to unsettle the lonely. Who would fend for them behind closed doors? Who sees them once they retreat into the privacy of their homes? I didn't mean to mistreat her, I just didn't like her.

"They were a hundred feet away from me," she said. "I didn't know what to do. Is that Leah? But Leah is in India, in Thailand, I don't remember where, she's in all kinds of places, but here? I didn't know if I should wave at her, maybe call out her name? She'll think I'm crazy. I waved. She didn't wave back. I wanted to shout, Leah! Leah! But I was too embarrassed. It wasn't her, it can't be. But a dead ringer! And then Rafi came running out of nowhere, and the bus driver called me back, and the woman, Leah, she approached the girls and took their hands and the three of them started walking away. I'm so sorry I didn't take her picture. You wouldn't believe it, Yoella. It was Leah. Everything about her, Leah."

I smiled. I managed to. I said, "That's some story."

I can't recount the next few days. What I can say is that I now knew where to look for my daughter, and I found her easily. She was living in Groningen. Married to Yohan Dappersma. They had two daughters, Lotte and Sanne. It would be a few months before I found a photo of Lotte online. I would find a photo of Yohan too. And a photo of the two girls together. And an eleven-second video from Sanne's birthday. And in that video, I would find Leah.

From my first day at the library I was careful not to make eye contact, especially with anyone coveting conversation. But the next time Art walked up to the checkout counter to pick up the books he had ordered, I returned his smile. I had noticed him before and knew that every so often he checked out books in German and Dutch. I wanted to travel to Holland, had already decided I would, but couldn't bring myself to just go. Not by myself. I needed him. I wanted someone to be waiting for me upon my return.

Those days, those long nights alone at home, without Meir and without Leah, I tried to pick up our trail again. Scouring my inbox I found a few short video clips I had sent myself years ago—the sudden memory of their existence spurring a frantic search. The videos were without sound, something had gone amiss over the years, but everything else remained as it had been. The chase. Leah crawling across the living room, her tiny behind ballooned in a giant diaper, Meir on her heels. Out of breath she stops, sits up for a moment to glance over her shoulder, then continues onward in startled delight. The father catches his daughter and together they roll around on the carpet, Leah's mouth agape in laughter. In another video she's sitting in a laundry basket with a pair of underwear on her head, and in yet another she is already seven years old and I'm handing her her first pair of glasses—I had picked them up from the optometrist's on my way home from work—and she puts them on carefully, lifts her gaze to me, and opens her mouth in astonishment.

Sometimes we cooked together. I pulled a chair up to the

kitchen counter and she stood next to me, stirring cake batter
or very carefully chopping vegetables; and if she nevertheless
ended up nicking herself, we tended to it calmly. Water, anti-
septic ointment, Band-Aid. She was proud of her Band-Aids,
wouldn't peel them off even when they turned gray. I have photos of her doused in flour. Photos with a doughy mustache. She's
doubled over in laughter in all of them. In a few of the photos
Meir makes a cameo. He's looking not at the camera but at his
daughter, his face suffused with love. In the photo still adorning
the fridge Leah leans forward, arms raised and face squirming
with joy. These are her first independent steps, from crawling to
walking, the intoxicating heights of the biped. Meir's arms outstretched toward her. I studied these photos over and over.
Without them it would have been impossible to believe. That
she was happy. That I did not make it up.

Who could I ask about us? Meir had died, Leah was gone.
Under no circumstances could I ask my mother. Everyone hunts
down their memories and mutilates them according to their
own design, my mother more than most.

I pored over the videos and photos every night, prying my
gaze away only when my eyes started stinging. I would lie on
the living room couch under the stream of my consciousness.
The summer Leah was four, she took a tattered toothbrush
under her wing. She made it a crib from an empty cheese con-
tainer and fed it from a filthy toy baby bottle with magically
never-ending milk. What was the doll's milk made of? It re-
pulsed me. I think I was worried that the bottle might break
one day. In the end I threw it away, and Leah searched for it

relentlessly until at last she gave up. She wouldn't stop consoling the toothbrush. Now I lay in the living room wondering— why did I throw it away? I did it for her, I didn't know any other way. I did it I without a second thought, but now I was filled with regret.

Retracing Leah's footsteps, I realized that in all those years when she was still beside me, I was lingering on her previous age, time always moved on, crushing memory under its heel. When she was five years old, I marveled at the photos of her when she was three. When she was seven, I struggled to remember what she was like at five. When she was ten, the baby she had once been completely faded from my mind. I didn't remember when she took her first step, when she started teething, how she parted with Carmella, her mangled rag doll that reeked of sweat and saliva. Unlike me, who didn't remember a thing, my mother remembered everything, not only about Leah, but about me too. She said, "You suffered miserably from ear and eye infections and caught colds from even the slightest whiff of winter." And she once told me, "Your first word was 'come.'" But it's only in a handful of the old photos that I can grasp her love for me. In one of them, my mother and I are on a blanket on the grass, she in a summer dress and her hair—which was always pulled back in a tight chignon—hanging loose about her shoulders. In the photo, she's supporting me with both hands, helping me stand, looking at me in part enchantment, part surrender, inconceivably young. She loved me; the difficulty lay in liking me. But stories about mothers and daughters are always in medias res, working backward to the beginning, even as there is no beginning. The path is simple yet crooked, the beginning slinks ever further away. As with the universe or numbers, there is no beginning.

One night I wake up with a start; my body is in shock. I was dreaming that I found out I had a fatal illness, an illness that had already taken me once by storm and had since slipped from my mind.

In all our years together I burdened Leah with my sadness only once. I couldn't shake the feeling that Meir was about to leave me, and I wouldn't sleep next to him. At night I would crawl into my daughter's bed; she would turn to me right away, wrapping herself around me with the perfect warmth of her body that offered its softness and asked for nothing in return. In Meir's arms I was always restless, whereas twelve-year-old Leah held me as if she knew all there was to know about human touch and how to calm me completely. That week I fell asleep beside her night after night, she was the cure for seven nights straight. We pulled through—I never found out what put an end to the affair, knew only that it was a student of his, perhaps I had seen her on campus, from afar, alone, and knew it was she. I knew as people often know. It was over, and I returned to our bed.

It was the following summer that I got pregnant. I was forty-three years old, Meir fifty-nine, and I told him with an excitement tinged with trepidation. I didn't know what his eyes were going to deliver until they delivered it. And so I terminated the pregnancy. I wasn't angry, I was relieved. Actually, I was angry.

But if I left Meir, what would I do with Leah? With whom would I love her? His drawn-out workdays, the trips and conferences, the quiet, fatherly, almost medical way he loved me continued after our daughter was born. I could keep going too. Besides, without Meir, with whom would I talk about Leah? To whom would I send the photos I'd taken of her? Share the funny things she said? Only Meir loved her as much as I did, was as interested in her as I was. Only in his eyes could I see the light snap on at the mention of her name. I couldn't leave him. I had Leah, I wouldn't be lonely, I knew that with Leah I would never be lonely again, and yet I still needed Meir, to see us. This was by no means a bad life, and it fit me.

42.

On a bench on my way to work rests a hefty book about women and madness. I pick it up and open it to a random page. *Painting after painting, sculpture after sculpture in the Christian world portray Madonnas comforting and worshiping their infant sons.* My gaze flips to the next page. *Female children are quite literally starved for matrimony: not for marriage, but for physical nurturance and a legacy of power and humanity from adults of their own sex.*

I had never heard of this book, which was left on the bench next to an electric kettle and a stack of back issues of a distinguished psychology magazine. I take the book and a couple of the magazines with me, but a few steps later change my mind, turn around and put them back. They have a smell that carries me back to my months of pregnancy, dust and spices and burned fat. But when I get home, I decide I'll return to the bench in the evening, and if the book is still there, I'll take it after all.

43.

Toward the end of tenth grade we are invited to a parent-student day at school. Meir won't be able to make it, he is in Germany at a conference, but I will be there and will even help out with the seating arrangements. Each family is to bring a favorite family dish, and ours will be the mushroom casserole my mother taught me how to make. We will be split into groups for an activity, Leah explains. Four kids and their parents at each table; we will read handouts, talk them over and answer questions. The food will wait until after.

On our way to school Leah is quiet. But she has been quieter than usual for the past few months, and there is nothing about this particular moment to give me cause for alarm. When we were getting ready to go, she was wearing a dress and boots and had tied her hair into something like a braid; then she went back to her room and reemerged in jeans and a sweatshirt. This time her hair was down, and her old sneakers were on. I didn't say anything, but now in the car I ask, "So how have you been?"

And she says, "Fine. Everything's okay."

Her hands are resting on her knees, red and cracked. Winterweathered. She has good skin, like mine, but in the winter her knuckles turn a raw red.

From here the remembering muddles. I don't want to make anything up. To avoid doing so, I have to forget everything I could not conceive at the time, to separate the layers of time, which is a problem. It is beyond what the mind can do.

When we entered the classroom, two girls were already there; the teacher came in right after us and instructed us what to move and do. We set to it, pushing tables from here to there and making a racket, and I felt—this had happened to me before—that I might fly off the handle, might lash out and tell them that tables can be lifted, they don't have to be dragged, but I didn't know what words to use. How to say it not as a reprimand. How to talk without embarrassing Leah. The screeching steel on tile sawed through my brain, and still I was civil, glanced at my watch and smiled. I did the math—Meir was already on the train. I knew he was landing in Munich and boarding a train to Augsburg—and why had he not texted me yet? The noise shook me out of focus and jogged loose the awareness that I was being ridiculous. Meir loved me, he loved us. In all our years together, it had happened only once, only one student over one winter, and when he came back to me, he came back to me wholly, what did I have to worry about? Maybe I was disappointed with myself, for having gotten in the habit of living with a little warning light blinking in my head around the clock, especially when his travels took him far away.

Everyone arrived almost at the same time, the classroom filling up in a way that negated hierarchy. It no longer mattered who came first, who set up and who carried, everyone stood around talking; and then Arza appeared and lunged at Leah with a hug, and for a moment it seemed that she had come alone, but then I saw her mother, who was as beautiful as her daughter but not as perky, more sober in her deportment. I smiled at her, gave a light wave. Our daughters' friendship extended to us, that applied to all of Leah's friends, but if Arza's mother even noticed me, she did not show it. She looked in my direction but not at me, and someone else—some other mother—tapped her shoulder and they launched into conversation. The cacophony in the classroom was unbearable. Chatter and merriment and the smell of so many people packed in one room. I was about to step out for a moment, get some fresh air in the hallway, maybe call Meir, but when I turned to face the door, there he was. Dennis. I remembered him from the photo Leah showed me on Facebook, the photo she would touch on the screen with her fingertips, then bring them to her lips to kiss them. The photo didn't show much, but what it did show was enough. The long yellow hair. The face that wasn't from around here. The teacher stood by the blackboard and asked for quiet. Quiet down please, she said, and then she started talking. Good evening, it's so good to see you all, the activities will begin in a moment. And then she said she would call out the groups and table numbers and would we please take our seats.

Today I know what happened, but that evening was a jumble. Meir neither texted nor called, and I was worried, deliberately worried; amid the classroom clamor, worry was a form of protection, even if I didn't know what we needed protection from. My gaze searched for Leah, who was standing across the room, next to Arza and her mother, and despite the crowding and the distance, I could see that my daughter was pale, that something was not right. The teacher continued to read off names, and while people moved about the room to assume their places, I saw Dennis rush in and walk up to the teacher, who gestured impatiently: not now. Enough. And again I looked at Leah, and without understanding I understood.

We take our seats at the table. Leah and I, Ronit and her mother, Ophir and his father. Dennis, who was supposed to sit with us—the teacher clearly called out his name in our group— is at a different table, which is why there are now nine of them and six of us. Did his parents not come with him? Is he here alone? I look for them but they are nowhere to be seen. Dennis is on his own. Free, like an orphan. I consider Leah sitting beside me. Her cracked hands are shaking and her eyes fill with tears. Taking her hand in mine under the table, I squeeze it until the tremors abate. Then the discussion around the table begins and it takes a good while before she can open her mouth to speak.

44.

After my first trip to Groningen, I went back. Went back twice, but I couldn't bring myself to go near the window again. It is the truth, I am telling it all. I stopped at the end of the street and turned around.

I knew where Yohan worked. I wrote him twice, to no avail, but I could find him and stand in front of him. I could leave him no choice. Who can hide in this day and age? No one. Especially if someone is looking for them.

My daughter's husband taught at a theater school by the east harbor, the Lancering Theater Academy, a jutting building of concrete and glass that conformed perfectly to the ashy sky above it. I sat down at the café across the street. Dozens of bicycles and a few motorcycles were parked outside the building, an eyeful of drama and steel with an extravagant, eerie silence looming over it, a disruption of the city's equilibrium. Every so often the Lancering students crossed the street and entered the café, sticking to the cheapest items on the menu. Espresso, soda, pastries. People can be so young sometimes. A boy with a nose ring and pink hair belted out a song while waiting in line at the counter, and I thought, how nonchalantly the future spreads out its nets, you don't realize it until it's too late. Three girls a table over got up to leave and hugged one another with willowy delight. Was that how Leah conducted herself in these parts? As if the world was hers for the taking? Hugging everyone and everything? She had been Yohan's student, and when I found her on the internet under her new name, I also found a photo of Yohan she had posted seven years earlier, with "my teacher" in Dutch written under it. And yet I still could not picture her sitting in this café, laughing carelessly, undoing her ponytail, flipping her hair and pulling it back into a ponytail like someone who knows herself inside and out. Yohan was fifteen years her senior, perhaps even older. I understood what he had to offer her.

When he finally exited the building, he was alone. Lanky in a winter jacket, carrying a leather briefcase, like the character of a country doctor. I recognized him easily. I had studied his photographs, knew what he looked like, but I had not realized how tall he was. I had paid the bill in advance so that I could get up and leave at any given moment, and now was that moment— I jumped out of my seat and crossed the street. He rounded the corner onto the main shopping avenue, and I followed him. We walked. I had done this before, years ago. For the duration of one dreadful winter, I had trailed Meir undetected; I got good at it. Yohan darted down the street and came to a halt at the bus stop, where he placed his briefcase on the curb and searched his pockets. I didn't slow my steps, I rushed along, waiting for my mind to shut down so I could move from thinking to doing, like with skydiving, and I was already in close range when he glanced up at me and I kept going, passed him, was gone. He had a face like a composite sketch, where the features don't quite add up. I imagined this worked on my daughter, the slight incongruity between his forehead and nose; his lips, which might have piqued her interest in a way she could not quite explain. But the notion that he didn't recognize me as Leah's mother was suddenly unfathomable, ludicrous. I wasn't just another person passing by, I was the mother, his daughters were my granddaughters, we were linked by a bond that could not fail to signify something. I had sent him letters, he knew I existed, knew I was looking for him, and yet when he saw me, his expression remained blank. To him I was just a woman going about her business. Then again, he was an actor; if he had wanted to, he would have known how to put on a face that cloaked his thoughts. I kept walking. Even back then I knew more about him and his daughters than he could imagine. From all the information gathered piecemeal in a myriad of ways, I had mapped out a mental picture of the three of them, and yet still I was fumbling in the dark. I was in the dark. He and the girls loved Leah and also held her tight. My heart racing, suddenly light-headed, I made it to the end of the street. Maybe I had walked too quickly, it all happened so fast, there was something wrong, I was too eager. I thought, tomorrow I'll talk to him, tomorrow I'll wait for him outside the building and approach him the minute he comes out. Today was just a warm-up, I decided, I was rehearsing. Back at the café, I sat until my legs stopped shaking. They were shaking so hard under the table that I had to stabilize them with my hands.

That night, when darkness descends, I am back in their neighborhood, wandering the streets surrounding their house.

The ice cream shop, the pharmacy, the playground. These are the slides my granddaughters slide down. This is the bench my daughter sits on while watching them. Here are the swings that propel them upward, the sand that pours into their shoes. From this merry-go-round Lotte once fell and bumped her head and was rushed to the hospital. Such things happen. The neighborhood was an old one, and it seemed peaceful, but that did not mean nocturnal men did not prowl it, and I had to trust that my daughter knew how to keep her daughters safe. I made it all the way to the school they attended, the bare bicycle racks, the modest basketball court that in the darkness and from afar resembled a pool. I walked along the low fence leading up to the gate, which was open. Everything was open to me. But I was afraid of attracting attention, and in any case I did not want to venture too far; I did not overdo anything, only ran my hand along the fence.

45.

When I first started searching for my granddaughters I stayed up whole nights. I was hoping I would find them. I was hoping I wouldn't. I understood the violation. I went to the same websites again and again, clicked the same records and same photos, searched every corner as if some old detail might suddenly present itself in a new light. I could find them at any given moment, and I did. Lotte Dappersma. Sanne Dappersma. They were five and six, and slowly growing up. Six and seven. Students at De Lange Brug, the long bridge. Students at the local conservatory. Lotte for guitar, Sanne for flute. Unearthing Yohan's Instagram account coincided with a case of bronchitis that kept me bedridden for days. The minutiae of their lives became mine for the taking, the pattern of the curtains in the girls' bedrooms, the dome of light cast by Lotte's reading lamp, Sanne's loopy handwriting and penchant for green hearts. Sanne appeared more lighthearted than her sister, slyer. A mischievous face. I thought that with her, it would be easier down the road. Neither of them resembled Leah in the slightest, not in their looks, not in their expressions, not in the type of woman tucked inside them, lying in wait for the future. Small straight noses. The golden flour hair that froze about their heads mid-flutter, alive like a puppy, stirring in me the desire to sniff it and dip my hand in it. And still I did not lose my mind. Now that I was in possession of my granddaughters in photographic form, I withstood the urge. I had already tracked down several of Lotte's classmates and a few parents—I knew what I was doing. I had also located two of her friends from the conservatory. The mother of one of the girls, Maria Kuch, posted a short video from the end-of-year recital. The camera lens was fixed on Maria, a small, sallow girl, a fellow flutist. I watched the first few seconds, then paused to compose myself. A whole hour went by before I watched the rest of it. Next to Maria, on the edge of the screen, was Lotte. Over and over again, ten times, twenty, more, as many times as I wanted.

A few weeks later, as if I had gone entirely unnoticed, was not even on their radar, as if tracking them down and watching them from afar was an impossibility, Yohan posted a video from Sanne's birthday party, and there was everyone. Lotte, Sanne, Yohan, Leah. Eleven seconds. I want to say that seeing my granddaughters in motion was more than I could bear. I am saying that I was crushed by the sight of Leah bunching Sanne's hair into her hands as she leaned forward to blow out the birthday candles. And just like that, they were her daughters in every way; the resemblance, which lay below their features, in deeper strata, triggered a tremor of recognition that slammed me to the ground. Days of high fever, fitful sleep, and jumbled thoughts ensued. Had she found God, had she joined a cult, had she surrendered to a force greater than herself . . . But she remained Leah, she was Leah, and she no longer wanted to be my daughter.

I come across the article in one of my internet deep dives and peer at it in alarm—as if I had snuck up to the window at Groningen again. "Dutch children are the happiest in the world." After that, I read about my granddaughters anything I can put my hands on: studies, surveys, essays. It had not crossed my mind until then that this was another way I could learn about their lives. From what I read, it appears that family is at the center of Dutch life, and yet Dutch girls are not an extension of their parents. It seems that from a young age they are free to venture outside the house alone and look after themselves; that in the lives of Dutch girls, there is no such thing as bad weather, only bad clothing; that spontaneity is valued and encouraged; and that since the ruckus of children at play is not regarded as a disturbance, they know how to make their voices heard.

I piece together a mental picture. No homework until they reach the age of ten, and they cycle as naturally as they walk. French fries they eat with mayonnaise, and instead of umbrellas they have big plastic ponchos, like giant bags with a hood, but are not keen on wearing them, they find it embarrassing. When one of them celebrates her birthday, the whole family is congratulated, and when they are older, they will greet their friends with three kisses on alternating cheeks. I read that the teenage pregnancy rate in the Netherlands is among the lowest in the world, as is alcohol use, and that Dutch girls are among the tallest on the planet.

46.

I did not sit at the café again. It was the transition from sitting to walking that had me faltering the day before, and I understood that. I decided to stand, but how? Doing what? I stopped at a distance from the building, thirty yards down the road, so I could view the comings and goings at the entrance but also watch the street go by, a blasé bystander, a woman waiting for the ordinary things people wait for, perhaps a friend running late. Two hours I stood and waited, anyone else would have packed up; my back ached, the strap of my bag dug into my shoulder, and when Yohan appeared, I started after him. I was careful this time. I moved without working myself up, to preserve my energy. I skulked behind him up to the bus stop, sidled past him, and stopped a few feet away. An older gentleman waiting for the bus turned to him and said something I couldn't make out, not that I would have understood in any case. My daughter's husband smiled at the old man and replied amiably; you could tell he was the kind of man who never let his manners lapse, Dutch through and through, it was hard to say where his etiquette ended and his personality began. I did not expect him to smile at me as well, I knew he wouldn't. I had planned on saying very little to him. Not to go overboard. I didn't want to become emotional, no tears, please God, no tears. There's something wrong with Leah. That was the first thing I would say. There's something wrong with her, she is a conundrum, my daughter is a conundrum. I was hoping he would not tell me about her right away, not forget his loyalties and slip up, that he would understand we were in it together, that I was testing him just as much as he was me. I wanted to say only what I had planned, that I am here and I will come again, that I will not stop trying, that I will come without questions and without conditions and without holding Leah's disappearance against her. But I won't leave her alone. I won't. I wanted to tell him, calmly, that his daughters were also my granddaughters. Are my granddaughters. And how much I would like to get to know them. In my hand I had a note with my phone number and address, and I approached, was standing right behind them, if I had wanted I could have slipped the note in his pocket and walked away. The old man was still chatting, and now I was close enough to hear him, a widowed voice, a lonely man pent up in the silence of his home for most of the day and in need of the street to be heard. Yohan was a model of patience; they talked, the old man pointed at his watch and grumbled, and when the bus appeared around the corner, they nodded at each other in righteous acknowledgment, as if it had finally arrived only by virtue of their wise insistence.

My flight was scheduled to depart from Amsterdam the following evening. At night, in my hotel in Groningen, looking at the flight itinerary, I worked backward to calculate the travel time. I could take the 4:48 p.m. train to Almere at the latest and continue from there. A thirty-minute taxi ride from the theater school to the hotel to pick up my suitcase, and another fifteen-minute ride from the hotel to the train station. I could wait for Yohan until half past three. The last two times he had left the building, it was after four—if he came out before, I would know it was for me.

He appeared at the entrance to the building at 3:19 p.m., lingered for a moment on the stoop, and looked out onto the street. Everything happens for a reason, whether one understands it or not doesn't make it any less true. He waited for a moment, giving me time to prepare. I didn't lose my composure when he started walking, I was familiar with his gait, and with all due respect, it was an actor's strut. In one of the productions he was in (I had read everything I could find about him), he played a demented woman's son who helps her track down her childhood sweetheart, a role that had earned him accolades—his breakthrough. *The breakthrough.* But who even attends the theater these days? He strode down the street, and not a head turned. I knew exactly how long it would take me to catch up to him, and decided that I would approach right after he rounded the corner onto the main street, not tap on his back or shoulder, only call out his name—Yohan. Like most Dutch, he probably had good command of English. I would call his name and say, I'm Leah's mother, I'm Yoella, and to make sure he understood, I would repeat: I'm Leah's mother. Whatever expression his face assumed would tell me everything I needed to know, a fleeting window onto his true feelings before it snapped shut, obscuring whatever he didn't want me to access. A group of girls walking in the opposite direction came between us, blocking him from view, but when I wove around them, he reemerged. Everything was going according to plan. It was about to be over. As he continued down the street, he didn't turn onto the main road as he had done the two times before, and I momentarily lost my balance, my foot turned under itself. In any other life I would have fallen flat on my face, but I was catapulted forward instead, breaking my fall with my hand. Nothing happened. I was fine and kept going. Why didn't he take the turn to the bus stop? His walk was the same as it had been the day before, and the day before that—decisive, resolute—only brisker. He was picking up speed, and I was panting. Then he slowed down, looked up, took a few more steps, and stopped at the entrance to a building. I saw him from behind, but he had lifted his gaze to one of the windows—there was no doubt in my mind this had happened—he lifted his gaze and my eyes followed, and I saw what I saw. I myself had once been a very young woman very much in love, and I understood right away. Yohan pressed the buzzer and leaned his weight against the door. A hulking European wooden thing, restricting access, a door that would expand in my mind long after I left. It slammed shut behind him.

47.

In her first few weeks of high school, Leah talks about her loves and losses with equal aplomb, as if she has walked this planet for many years and garnered all the self-deprecating humor a woman needs to wade through life.

"Dennis doesn't give two hoots about me," she says, "he doesn't even see me."

"Dennis is an idiot," I tell her. "A big blind moron."

She laughs and mimics the way he flicks his head sideways to shake his hair from his eyes.

"And you're a moron too," I say. "A match made in heaven."

She puts on a serious expression. "But it's not *really* a crush anymore."

"I know."

"It's just for fun."

"A crush on crushing," I say.

"Yes."

"A training crush. Like a training bra, only with a crush."

"Exactly," she says. "Whatever, I'm an idiot, but listen, are you listening? I have a fantasy that's real but a fantasy."

My brow knits.

"I'll explain," she says. "I saw him writing in class, okay?"

"Dennis?"

"Focus, Mom. Who else would I be looking at in class? I saw him writing, but not in his notebook, on a piece of paper, and I realized he was writing me a letter. Okay. But at recess he didn't give it to me. That's weird, admit it. So I realized he's a little shy, that maybe he's nervous, because he wrote that he loves me and that's understandably embarrassing. I knew he'd give me the letter by the end of the day, but I forgot that I had to leave school early because of that tooth-cleaning appointment. And now he must be totally bummed out. But it's not the end of the world, he'll give it to me tomorrow."

"Really?"

"What do you think? It's a fantasy."

I slapped my forehead.

"Never mind, I'm an idiot. Deal with it. Your daughter is kind of dense. Did you buy batteries for my toothbrush? The dental hygienist told me to keep up the good work."

The transition to high school is smooth in every way. My daughter is one of those learning-hungry, hand-raising girls whose only sin is overeagerness. She's too much, and even this her teachers find delightful. They are wrong, of course. Her eagerness is exactly the thing that might tip the scales. Over the next few years, I will find myself saying: stay home today, just one day, what could happen? I'll stay in with you, we'll curl up on the couch, order pizza, watch a movie, and she'll roll her eyes and say, you want a day off, Mom? Take it. You don't need me for that. I will forever hear about girls who need reminders, a guiding hand, a gentle nudge in the right direction, whereas Leah I would only have to temper. Only temper a little. Console her when a grade is slightly less sterling than the last. Cajole her into having another piece of cake, or taking a short break from hours hunched over her textbooks. Go have some fun. I will insist that she learn to forgive herself. Forgive yourself, Leah. And if every now and then I'll see a shadow from my own youth cross her face, a glimpse into the recesses of her soul, I will wait with her until it recedes.

One after the other, the holidays blow by. Rosh Hasha-
nah, Yom Kippur, Sukkot, Simchat Torah. The clus-
ters of vacation days throw Leah off-balance, and as
soon as school is back in session, barely two days in, she decides
she wants to ask Dennis to be her boyfriend. She consults with
Meir, who advises her to wait a little longer. The year has only
just begun, he says, you've only just met, give it time. It seems
that she's giving his advice serious consideration.

But that very night she shuffles out of her room and says, "I
asked him. I texted him. But he didn't answer."

My heart freezes. "He probably hasn't seen it yet," I blurt.

"It's okay," she says. She doesn't have more to add on the
matter, and even later, when I enter her room to give her a bedtime kiss, it is not the hardest day of her life. Her spirits are high.
My mind loops back to her childhood fevers, the electrical
storms of her speech. When I get up at three in the morning to
go to the bathroom, I see through a chink in her door that she
has turned on the fairy lights. In the glow of the gold and turquoise balls she looks asleep, but I know she only closed her
eyes because she heard my footsteps.

The next day, I am in the middle of a meeting at the studio when she calls me, sobbing. I excuse myself and step out.

She is calling from the girls' bathroom. Dennis still hasn't talked or written to her. He's been ignoring her all day. But it is not a desperate cry, I can hear the relief it carries. Only hours later, long after evening has fallen, he texts her: "No . . . sorry."

The following evening, Arza shows up at our house, and they shut themselves in Leah's room. The next day, after school, Leah goes home with Arza and stays there until dinner. Arza's parents go up north for the weekend, and she invites Leah for a sleepover. It will be just the two of them, big girls. I am constantly checking my phone. She does not call or write once that whole day and night. Saturday afternoon, so that she won't hear the tremor in my voice, I text her and she replies right away. "Everything's fine." Saturday night she is back home and it seems that she has put her sorrow behind her.

The year goes on.

They form a small group: Leah, Arza, another girl, named Gal, whose name now often features in Leah's stories, and two boys, Misha and Miko.

"Miko?" I ask.

"Eylon Mikoshinsky."

Misha is most likely gay, Leah says. But he doesn't know it. And he's sweet. No particular observations are made about Miko. The girls call one another darling, and the boys call Leah and Arza Leli and Razi, and turn Gal into Gala.

"Miko says a name can't have just one syllable," Leah explains; "he says it's inhumane."

"That bad?"

"You wouldn't get it."

Misha calls Miko Miko, whereas Miko calls Misha Marko.

"Marko?!"

"Never mind." Leah cuts me short.

She's under the spell of their little group, which for the first time includes boys, an exciting new world of tunnels and chambers. The girls coax the boys into games of rates and comparisons. Who do you like the most in class? Who do you want to kiss? Who do you think is the prettiest? They are also required to pick second and third places, at first a little randomly and later with conviction, and finally they must also pick last place. Last place brings on a flurry of excitement. It is akin to asking them to name the ugliest, most repulsive girl, a girl who grosses them out. I know they also play Truth or Dare and that they are not particularly interested in dares, only the truth enthralls them. I myself was always scared of those games, still am.

Dennis, who had dissipated into nonexistence, now rematerializes in Leah's stories. "He actually talks now, sometimes," she says. Sometimes he answers the teacher's questions, and he's always drawing in class. He has a sketchbook, and at recess he left it open on his desk and Leah stole a peek. She told him his drawings were amazing and he blushed and said thank you. The next day, when she and Misha stayed behind in the classroom at recess to play Taki, he glanced at them, and she asked if he wanted to play. He said no. But the day after that, he approached of his own accord and joined them.

Arza doesn't like Dennis—ever since their days in choir, more adamantly since he turned down Leah's overture—but because Leah likes him, the rest of the group is nice to him, and within no time at all, he's one of them, and Leah no longer discloses much, not about him or any of the others.

S ummer break sweeps in with a lingering silence. First Arza goes away with her family to Europe, and before their return, Meir, Leah, and I travel to Minnesota. Meir is teaching a summer course at a small lakeside college, which has set us up with a comfortable apartment on campus. During Meir's morning lectures, Leah and I borrow bicycles from the neighbors and cycle to the lake. We spend the rest of our time ambling along the main shopping street, rummaging through the local bookshops and clothing stores, and planning the dinners we will prepare in our little apartment. We take a liking to a tiny noodle place tucked into one of the smaller streets and run by a few Asian women—not a man in sight—and when I ask one of the women about this, her English suddenly evaporates. The others also fall mute. They are not interested in conversation. Leah, who for some time now flinches every time I strike up a conversation with strangers, doesn't say anything but is visibly mortified.

"What?" I say when we're alone at the table again. "What did I do?"

"Nothing."

"What is it?" I ask. "Did I talk too much? Did I breathe too quickly?"

"Stop it, Mom, you're like a child."

She has reached the age where she has invented everything herself, including maturity.

A short time after our arrival in Minnesota she befriends a boy named Oliver, the son of visiting lecturers from England, with whom she plays Frisbee on the campus quad and goes for ice cream on the main shopping road. Ollie is short and cheerful, and when he isn't around, she allows herself to swoon over him, but in his presence she is quiet and apprehensive. The burden of conversation therefore rests with Ollie, who is not unnerved by prolonged silences. They sit outside the ice cream shop, licking their cones while scrolling their phones before a quiet walk back to the campus.

When we return to Israel, there are still two weeks of vacation left before the school year begins. Surprisingly, Leah doesn't head straight out to see her friends, and none of them appears at our door. When I ask her about it, she shrugs and says she rather likes the quiet, being at home. She says she will soon have a whole year with them, there's no rush.

We spent only six weeks in Minnesota, but it feels as if we were away for years. Everything in our home has become time-worn and downsized. I cannot get the place to look clean, no matter how hard I scrub it. But a few days go by and it seems fine again.

48.

The writer who wrote about Juliet has disclosed that she might now retire from writing. She is over eighty years old, and I think that perhaps it is difficult for her to continue; all those characters, the heartaches, the disasters. But maybe putting down her pen will prove even harder. She titled the story I'm reading now "Child's Play," and I start by skimming the first few pages to guess what kind of game awaits me. *Girls nine or ten years old . . . somebody I didn't know . . . used a special voice . . . so narrowly built and with such a small head that she made me think of a snake.* I go back to the title page and start from the beginning.

Apparently, the writer took no mercy on the playing girls, or on anyone around them. Again and again their heads get pushed under the story's waves, leaving them gasping for breath.

Three days before the new school year, I take Leah to the mall to buy everything we haven't bought yet. She wanders around the store, weaving between rows of backpacks, pencil cases, and pads of paper, ruling out everything that looks nice to me:

"Atrocious . . . Lord have mercy . . . Are you for real?"

She picks a glossy yellow pencil case and a very blue lunch box. The notebooks are red, the binders green. She seems to be doing it on purpose. One by one she plucks the ugliest items off the shelves and plops them into her shopping basket.

Without a word, I pay for everything.

"Are you mad?" she asks in the car on our way home.

"Mad? Why?"

"You hate all my picks."

I say, "No, no, no. Not at all."

"You think they're ugly."

"Let's not exaggerate. Ugly's a big word. It's just stuff."

Leah gives me a tentative look.

"You hate all my picks."

"I do not."

49.

Puberty sets in subtly. Leah is prone to crying over the tiniest things but she is not petulant, showing only random displays of impatience—the usual matryoshka doll of moods, typical of teens. She is a reasonable, sweet, thoughtful adolescent, and if it happens that she snaps at me, she is quick to appease. I'm sorry, Mom. Don't be mad. I apologize. I'm sorry. Do you forgive me?

Some mornings her eyes are swollen from crying or sleeplessness. She asks the same questions over and over again without listening to the answer, then a few moments later asks them again. She reminds me of my mother after my father's passing, but my mother I punished with my tone of voice or an eye roll, whereas for my daughter I repeat myself calmly. I say, yes, of course I'll buy you that lotion. No, I haven't heard about that movie. I don't see why not, I say. Whatever you want, I say, I'll come get you.

The fall holidays come and go again. The first rain washes over a long summer of parched trees, houses, and streets. One winter evening, as we sit around the table eating, I ask her about her chapped hands. I already noticed a few weeks ago that they seemed worse than usual, so why didn't I ask then? What was I thinking?

"They're so itchy," Leah says, scrunching up her sleeves to show me the sticky scratches running the length of her arms, "it's driving me crazy." Afterward, when she steps out of the shower, I offer her a soothing ointment and leave it at that.

The winter draws to a close, and one night, when I go into her room to tuck her in and turn off the light, she sits up and asks me to stay.

"To sit with you?"

"Yes."

And she bursts into sobs that send her whole body shaking.

I toss and turn in bed the whole night. I want to tell Meir everything but am afraid Leah might hear us through the wall. When she cried, I held her gently. She wanted to tell me everything so that I would know, for the sake of knowing and nothing more; she did not ask for solutions. She glowed with a cold white light, very different from the febrile light of her childhood illnesses, and it wrenched my heart. Maybe that is when I first wanted Dennis to disappear, I don't remember. I would like to think I never wanted that, never wished for it.

L isten."

And I do.

At the end of the summer, Leah tells me, when she felt she and Dennis were already close, already friends, she worked up the nerve again.

"I asked him again," she says. "I told him, I love you and I want to be your girlfriend."

This time he answered straightaway, and she put on a bold face, and only afterward, in the girls' bathroom, let the tears flow freely.

"But I'm fine now."

"When was this?" I ask.

"Mom—"

She starts wailing again. I hug her. In the months that followed, she tells me, if she sat down next to him in the circle of kids playing card games at recess, he got up and changed places. If the teacher assigned them to the same study group, his hand shot up and he asked to change groups. If he caught her eye on him, he told her, stop looking at me, you're embarrassing me, you disgust me, leave me alone. Don't look at me, he told her, don't look at me at all. Ever. I wish you'd just get out of my face.

When she is done speaking, I search her face and eyes, but there is only sorrow there, the ice burn that blistered her heart. I do not understand what my daughter is made of. I love her with an unbearable, perhaps impossible love, and him I loathe in the same manner.

50.

I send the letter on my way to the airport. On a white piece of paper I had written down the address of the building Yohan ducked into, nothing more. I added in Dutch, "Your husband has been visiting here," and included the address. Nothing more. I scrawled the letters from bottom to top, such that no one could possibly guess the handwriting was mine. Then I bought an envelope and a stamp and slipped the letter into a mailbox nowhere near a post office—rendering it irreparably beyond my reach by the time I changed my mind.

On the flight back, muddled with exhaustion, I down two mini vodka bottles before dozing on and off. I have sent something out into the world and am awaiting its return. My daughter is a conundrum but not to me. I knew her then and know her still. She will need one person in the world who loves her more than anything.

51.

The stores are brimming with things for girls, and I find everything lovely and want to buy it all. I had a co-worker once whose husband had a half brother who came here for a visit, a sixty-year-old bachelor, Italian, but not from a well-known place, from some town in the south, Tripea or Tropea. "Good-looking," she said, "but doesn't shut up." And he brought gifts for everyone. Whisky for his brother and perfume for my friend, a nifty little glider for their eleven-year-old and a toy train for their four-year-old. But for the daughter, she said, her nine-year-old, her middle child, he brought a bathing suit and a gleaming boxed set of Disney princess underwear. My friend didn't know what to make of it. Afterward, whenever her daughter wore the bathing suit, it made her skin crawl. The underwear she tossed in the garbage can.

In everything I buy for my granddaughters, there is a message I have to decipher beforehand, which is why I can only buy things without hidden compartments, insinuations, echoes. No clothes; whatever I buy has to be at a safe remove from the body. No dolls. No books. No toiletries. At the stationery shop, I buy two pricey backpacks and a few attractive notebooks, but later, doubts creep in even about these. The backpacks are a burden, and the empty notebooks will have to be filled.

Two weeks after my last trip to Groningen, Yochai and I meet again. He does not ask about Leah. Perhaps he already understands, although it is more likely that she simply has not crossed his mind. He tells me about the woman he has met. Really nice, he says. He still has not told Danit about her, but he intends to, soon. Anyway, he says, he is happy. He is happy and he is having a nice time with the nice woman. He considers me, and since I do not ask, he leaves it at that. He tells me about Danit, about a problem she is having with one of the teachers at school. He seems more relaxed than in our previous meetings, which means that he is already sleeping with the nice woman, and that is fine. The image of a naked Yochai should not come as a surprise to me. Some women—women I could even like—find his type charming, a touch of the bohemian in his high forehead, the white hair combed back in a plush wave. And the tone of his voice attests to his attentiveness. But when I try to picture his private parts, basic yet astonishing, they belong to the worlds of other women leading other lives.

I have little interest in Yochai's late-blooming, and perhaps only now understand that he kept his distance from me all those years in order to protect me. Maybe he was afraid he wouldn't be able to keep Meir's secrets from me, and it makes me want to tell him, reassure him, that I knew everything. That I have lived in the world. That I knew when Meir pulled away and when he came back, and I took what I could.

A whole hour passes, and finally I glance at my watch and apologize that I must be on my way. I have to go pay my mother a visit, I say, she isn't feeling well. I decide I will not see him again.

I wait. I bent a string in the world and I'm waiting for the consequences of my actions.

Days go by, weeks. Seventy-six days. When the phone rings, I pick up without panic, take it to the bedroom, and quietly close the door.

"Hello?"

Art is in the living room, watching TV. The house is peaceful. I don't turn on the light in the room, I'm at ease in the dark. I sit down on the edge of the bed.

"Mom?"

I don't want her to torment herself. I never meant to torment her, and now I tell her, Liki, Liki, listen to me. Whatever you're afraid of telling me, I've already figured out and I know. None of it matters anymore. I can come over right away. I'll come, get a hotel room, I'll be close by, I'll be there for you. Anything you want.

The next morning, I go see my mother. Weeks ago, the two of us went to buy her a hearing aid, the best one out there, but she refuses to wear it. She reads a lot, or sits in front of the TV, watching movies, she can make do with the subtitles. Since she no longer wants to leave the house, I swap library books for her, and when the ones I pick aren't to her liking, she doesn't say, boring, banal, mindless. She says, too heavy, too sad.

This time, as soon as I enter, she asks, how is Art. She recently met him at my house. I invited her over for dinner, and they took a liking to each other. He's doing great, I say, busy. I'll make us tea, I say, and she nods and smiles. Maybe all these years, it was her hearing that was weighing on her.

I stand in the kitchen with a view of her back and speak in a whisper, not to startle her. Leah is in Holland, Mom. She met a man there, has two girls. But now something awful has happened to her, her husband is cheating on her and she'll be moving back here. I add two teaspoons of sugar to her tea, my mother has retained her sweet tooth, that hasn't changed, and with her back to me, she shakes her head lightly. From the kitchen she appears plainer, sitting in her armchair, her white hair still pulled into a tight chignon, her slightly stooped back pressed against the velvet backrest. I come into the living room and serve her the tea, which she drinks in measured sips. If she heard even a single thing I said, she never lets on.

52.

I 'll tell on him," Arza says to Leah one day. "I'll say he har-
assed me. He'll get kicked out of school and we won't have
to see him anymore."

Leah shakes her head. No no no. "Quit it. Just stop, stop being ridiculous." As much as she wants him to disappear, the
thought of his absence paralyzes her. Dennis is the source of her
suffering but also her joy, and Arza, who understands this as
only girls their age can, is willing to make the decision for her.
All or nothing? My daughter's friend has already decided, it's
just a matter of time.

For weeks now, Leah has been waking up every night and
can't fall back asleep. The itching in her arms has worsened, and
her neck too is dappled in red splotches. Maybe it's the dryness,
she says, maybe it's from the cold. She always suffered in the
winter, the problem of her frozen fingers was a constant in our
lives, but those splotches are new.

At recess, despite the blustery weather, she rushes out of the
classroom to the farthest corner of the yard, where Dennis
never goes, and when she returns to class, her heart is pounding
with the fear of bumping into him. Arza doesn't leave her side,

does her best to look after her and cheer her up. Sitting with her in the schoolyard, she tells Leah about the horrible, misery-laden life awaiting Dennis from here on, and sometimes, while Leah is crying, a laugh will find its way in. "Karma is a bitch," Arza says, handing Leah a tissue, and now they're both laughing. But on more difficult days, they can't come up with anything funny, neither of them, especially given that now, at recess, Leah sometimes withdraws to the library, sits in front of an open book and pretends to read. She wants to be alone, at least sometimes, and so as not to hurt Arza, she plies herself with books.

When the classroom door opens to the dawning disaster, Leah and Arza still share a desk, but Arza already spends most recesses with Gala and Misha, and by now rarely follows Leah to the yard or the library. They're no longer inseparable, and in fact, that day, during the two last periods, Arza has disappeared from class without a word to Leah.

In the doorway stands the school counselor, Diana. She asks the teacher to step outside for a moment, and the teacher walks out and back in not a second later, saying, "Leah, Diana is waiting for you in the hallway."

When Leah is ushered to the principal's office, she passes by the open door to the counselor's office, where Arza is sitting next to a woman she's never seen before. Is she crying? Why is Arza crying? Leah lingers there for a split second. Arza meets her gaze, and with the subtlest tilt of her friend's chin, Leah understands exactly what's going on.

The rest unfolds in less than a minute. In addition to the principal, the grade-level coordinator is also sitting in the office.

They haven't involved the police yet, which is why they are under no obligation to notify us, the parents. The air in the principal's office is heavy with the smells of pencil and of paper hot from the copier, mingled with the aftershave emanating from the principal himself, and Leah, who has lost considerable weight over the past weeks, is feeling woozy. The grade-level coordinator asks her to take a seat, she has a few questions she needs to ask.

On such-and-such date, did Arza tell her that Dennis hurt her in some manner?

"Yes," Leah says.

Did she tell her what he did?

"No," Leah says.

There are no more questions. The counselor thanks her, and she's dismissed back to class.

All this Leah divulges only weeks later, and even though she tells me everything, I can't understand. She is sobbing so hard that every so often I have to ask her to repeat a word or a sentence. I have never seen anything like it, the tears are magma surfacing, something immense has gone down and my daughter is devastated. Meir appears at the door to her room. What happened. What happened. But he is not needed here now; I gesture him away and he understands, this isn't the first time she has cried and wanted only me. I close the door after him and sit down beside her on the bed. What exactly is she saying? What is she telling me? I don't understand. I understand, but not the what and how of it, and then somehow I do. She lied? She lied to the principal? About what? When?

I listen to everything, agree to everything. I say, everything will be okay, everything is okay, and nod in reassurance. What do I say to her? For the first time in her desolations I'm at a loss for words. I understand what she has done, what she has instigated in the world. It all happened seven weeks ago, and Dennis was immediately suspended from school; for three weeks, they said, she isn't sure, but he hasn't returned. She expected him to be back, waited for him to be back, but he didn't come back. On and on she sobs, she never imagined this would happen, she had no idea, she'll go to the principal and explain, she has to. "Don't tell Dad," she implores once she is calmer and has exhausted herself from crying. "He'll be so mad at me." I tighten the blanket around her, cup her cheek, and kiss her forehead. Later, in the living room, I tell a concerned Meir, "Boy problems. She's calmed down, I calmed her down." But a few hours later, I wake with a start, staring into the abyss beneath us. I rush to her room. She's awake, she's lying awake in the darkness, and I tell her, I thought about it, Leah, listen to me. You won't do anything and you won't say anything. Enough time has gone by, his suspension is over, he can come back if he wants, it's his decision. They asked you, you answered, it's done. You go on with your life. You just go on with your life. And she's crying again and I get into her bed and hug her, and she sinks into a turbulent sleep.

53.

Dennis was seen wandering around town during the day. He was spotted sitting in Cats Square at night. He was sighted ascending from the Valley of the Cross at dawn, entering the Old City at sunrise, riding a motorcycle through Ein Kerem. These were always second- and thirdhand reports, and I advised Leah not to believe them. Not to be so quick to believe everything. People talk, they like talking. Look at him. Look at what happened to Dennis. We knew him, he was one of us and looked like us but he wasn't really, he was cut from a different cloth.

Leah refuses to let go. On an almost weekly basis she hunts for new rumors about Dennis to drop at my feet. Word has it that he decided not to return to school after his suspension and instead enrolled in a high school diploma program, before dropping out of that too. It was rumored that he was doing drugs, that his parents had kicked him out, that he was sleeping in a cave outside the city with a group of drifters—all this she tells me with swelling emotion, with an excitement I can't quite make sense of. Something of her old electrical storms has come back, that voice that cuts through the fog. With these stories she both frightens and sustains herself, it's not entirely clear to me how.

In this circumstance, I have to make myself heard. It didn't leave him with a criminal record, I shout. He didn't have to face charges, no one ruined his future. He was suspended from school, that's all. What happened happened, you don't know exactly what occurred and you never will. He was suspended for three weeks and decided not to come back, and if he wants to destroy his life, that's his business, and entirely up to him. It doesn't have anything to do with you, let it go. I'm actually yelling, that's happening too, and afterward I run my hand over her hair and speak into her eyes, and so we carry on. She is now almost as tall as I am, has suddenly shot up overnight, and her new height beguiles us both. Every so often she dives back into her studies and other pursuits, quiet and busy, then suddenly bobs up, arms outstretched for a hug, and presses herself against me. Or she's relaxing in front of the TV, staring at the screen, and I have to call out her name over and over again until she answers. Or she comes into our bedroom and lies beside me with a book in her hand or headphones over her ears, silent. I know her, no one knows her better, she needs my closeness to summon the strength to move forward, but then, in the blink of an eye, my soothing effect fades and she's swept back up into the storm. But I lied, she says in a flat voice. Mom, they asked me and I lied. And then she says she'll go to the counselor and tell her. That she'll go to the principal and tell him. That she has to, she has to tell someone. Dennis didn't do anything to Arza, she says, he didn't harass her. Arza made it up, and she, Leah, backed her up, and for that she has to be punished.

Deserves to be punished. She has to tell, she reiterates, and she will.

"Then do it," I say.

"I will."

"Go on," I say, "tell whomever you want. There's the phone right there, do it now, call the whole world."

"I'll tell," she says.

But she says this only to me, only when it's just the two of us home, without Meir, so I can stop her. So I can try, first with sarcasm, then with softness, then finally by grabbing her arm too tightly and yelling, enough, Leah, enough. You're not responsible for this. You were asked and you answered. You had your friend's back. You did what you thought was the right thing, and if it was me, I'd have done the same. Do you remember the damage that boy did to you? How miserably he treated you? He was cruel. He said awful things to you, he humiliated you in front of everyone. And he was suspended because he had to be, if not for Arza, then for you, and that's what matters. And that's why you won't go to anyone and won't talk to anyone and won't go stirring up what's over and done with, you understand? Do you? And sometimes I tell her, you know what? You don't believe Arza but I do. You're not the center of the universe, not everything revolves around you, not everything is yours and in your control. You don't know everything. How could you? Understand your place in the world, Leah. This isn't yours. Forget about it. Move on.

When doubt starts creeping in, I find my way to the student records. It's even easier than I could have hoped for; the school secretary is overcome with gratitude when I volunteer to spend the afternoon helping print out song sheets for the Purim party, and as soon as she leaves for the day, I rummage through her desk, where in the top drawer, next to a bottle of hand lotion and mints, lie the keys to the filing cabinet. The homeroom teacher has written pages upon pages about Dennis, I don't have time to read it all—I promised the secretary I would leave before the janitors finished their shift—but this boy clearly kept her busy. Other teachers also mentioned social issues. Sits alone during recess. An avid reader, but also prone to getting into fights. The counselor's ninth grade report notes a "hot temper" and "anger management problems," highlighting in red ink a fistfight between him and a classmate that resulted in the classmate's broken arm and a three-day suspension for Dennis. All this happened the previous year, in ninth grade, when Leah was already lovestruck and would come home from school with her eyes sparkling and her heart open like a sunflower stretching to the light. *He's so cute, Mom. You cannot believe the cuteness.* My skin crawls when I remember the singsong of her voice, how it scaled up when she spoke of him. How did she not tell me about that suspension? She must have known about the fight and felt his absence. She must have worried about him. Maybe she was embarrassed to tell me.

I want to know about the parents. I want to know what they are capable of, how far their reach is. I learn that the beautiful mother is from Moscow, whereas the father, whom I saw at the parent-teacher conference, is in fact not the father at all but the mother's brother. So everything makes sense, I think. Such a boy can experience challenges, can himself become a challenge. It was in everyone's interest that he be removed, and even more so that he decided not to return. It is a shame that it came to this, I think, but so it is.

Only once did I threaten Leah. Truly scared her. Quietly, calmly, I told her, okay. Do what you want. If you want to talk, talk. Go to the principal, come clean, tell him you lied. I'll stand by you no matter what, I'll help you through it.

I knew her, I knew exactly what I was doing.

"What will happen to me?" she asked.

"I don't know." I sidled up next to her on the bed. "Do you know what perjury is? Do you know what could happen if you went to the principal now? You falsely accused him, do you understand that? Do you understand what that means? Tell me you understand, that's all."

"But I'll save him," she said. "Don't you see what this is about? I caused this, I lied and I'm going to fix it."

I kept my voice calm and composed. Very composed. "That boy made you miserable," I said. "He was cruel to you. He was always a menace, and now you see exactly who he is and what he's made of. Look what happened to him, how quickly he spiraled. You can't save him from himself, but if you confess now, you might inflict horrible damage to yourself. As long as you understand this, it's fine. If you have to, do it. We'll handle it, come what may."

"And you?" she asked. "If I confess, will you forgive me?"

I didn't answer. I got up and walked out of her bedroom.

I waited. Over the following days I thought about it constantly, held it all in, it's hard to explain. Like a criminal waiting to get caught. And the pacts I had made—if all goes well this week, if nothing goes down the next. I promised things I later forgot about, I made light of them. It happens, you forget the intensity of the intent. The phone would ring in the morning and I would think, don't let it be from school. Don't let it be Leah. But as the days went by, I didn't become more grateful, I became angrier. I was angry at Leah. She was putting my daughter in danger. Leah was putting Leah in danger. It might sound as if I was deranged, but I became sharper. I saw everything very clearly. The fact that she even thought about talking. That she had considered harming herself in that way. And for who? For what? And when she came home in the afternoon, or in the evening, I'd look for signs. Did she talk to anyone? Go to the principal? The counselor? Confide in someone? I investigated without interrogating, only what I could see or gather. And the days passed. One at a time.

It was around then that my mother's hearing problems began. A litany of tests had to be run, and my mother, who had treated doctors with such deference throughout her years as a nurse, with a groveling that I couldn't bear, just like that, she became sick of them. There was a long, unsettled score whose details were unknown to me, reserves of animosity or distress that had piled up in another time and place and were now erupting, and to keep her calm I had to accompany her to every test. Every week or two I'd leave the studio early to take her to some clinic or medical center, where we would sit side by side in the waiting room, drinking vending machine coffee, and wait. We would talk, flip through old magazines and show each other articles. We killed time. It was a good partnership, we were closer than usual, as if the possibility still existed. And I remember wanting to tell her, thinking, I'm going to tell her, I can do it, I just need to find the right moment and take it from there. But I didn't tell her. In the end, there's no denying it, I didn't tell. Maybe at just the opportune moment she went over to the water fountain or turned to the stack of newspapers, and the door closed. I couldn't cross the threshold. And so the ride back was spent discussing what the doctor said and what needed to be done next.

That day was a long one. There was terrible traffic on the way back, and when the fuel light flashed on, I pulled into the first gas station that came along. There was a line there too, and my mother sighed her distress. Every medical exam sapped her, left her depleted and impatient. There was another station nearby, a short stretch down the road, but when I tried to back out, I saw that another car had already pulled up behind us; we were stuck. We waited a few more minutes and finally crawled up to a pump. And when I reached back to get my wallet out of my bag, I saw him. At first glance I couldn't be sure, but my heart was already thrumming with certainty. He was standing there in his attendant's uniform, talking to an older woman through her car window. He was still beautiful, but he had faded, his color off. Still talking to the woman, he pointed to something I couldn't see, then suddenly lifted his head and looked straight at me. And the fact that he looked up and found me without searching at all, as if he had been waiting for me— there was that too, I now realize. It's the way you hate someone and wait for them to cross your path. He didn't take his eyes off me. He approached us and I rolled down my window, and had my mother not been sitting next to me I would have met his gaze, we would have locked eyes—but I looked away. What if he said something, anything? I said, "A full tank, please," and handed him my credit card. He considered the card, glanced at the name, and looked at me. From the side-view mirror I followed his movements, tracked the execution of each and every one. He came back with my card and the slip, his eyes on me, no one had ever stared at me like that. I signed, handed him back the slip, and rolled up the window. And then, from behind the glass, he touched me. With just his fingertip, he touched the windshield. I turned to my mother. Her eyes were closed, she had dozed off. My heart banged wildly as I drove off.

54.

My mind flashes back to a girl I had forgotten about. When I was in sixth grade, a girl from my class was killed in a car accident. She lay injured in the hospital for two weeks, then died of her wounds. Maybe there's a word for that, for a lingering death. Anyway, she was there one moment, gone the next. We were notified of her death during history class, in the middle of the Normandy invasion and its thousands of casualties, and this death of a single girl we knew cut into our consciousness; all at once, there was a transcendence to it, something independent of reality and surpassing it. Many of us burst into tears. It was contagious, I cried too. Shocked, we walked the school hallways—it was too cold and rainy to go outside—feeling that we had been chosen somehow, for what I don't know, but that we had become more important than we were before. We went to the shiva in bands of five or six and with great intention, but when we got there the scale tipped, she was no longer ours at all, the parents' grief was impenetrable.

55.

Two days after I saw him at the gas station, Dennis's motorcycle plunged off the winding ascent at the entrance to Jerusalem. A special rescue vehicle spent hours maneuvering cables down the rocky slopes and into the wadi to extract what was still extractable. Traffic was backed up all the way to Shaar Hagai.

I heard about it on the evening news. "The name of the casualty in the motorcycle accident at the entrance to Jerusalem earlier today has been released . . ."

When I finally went into Leah's bedroom, she was sitting at her desk, scribbling away.

"Liki . . ."

She looked up at me with an expression I hadn't seen coming. She said, "I heard." And then she said, "I have a big history test tomorrow, okay? Call me when dinner's ready," and lowered her eyes back to her notebook.

We didn't talk about it again.

She went to Dennis's house for the shiva. I knew she had gone, I saw it on her face when she got back. She must have been afraid to go, or maybe her guilt was so great it eclipsed her fear, or perhaps she was praying for punishment. But I doubt anyone approached her, she was just one more girl amid a group of teens who had arrived at the home of the mourners only to realize that the grief of the mother and uncle was as sealed off to them as Dennis's death.

Speculations abounded. They always do. They said that he was high or drunk. That the night before the accident, he told a boy he smoked with in Cats Square that he was thinking about embracing religion. They said a witness told the police Dennis was speeding—racing like an absolute maniac—and suddenly flew with his bike into the sky and shot back down like a meteorite.

In the days and weeks that ensue, she holes up in her room after school for hours on end. From the moment she comes home, she sits at her desk studying or listening to music on her headphones. Her academic performance shines as brightly as ever, the teachers are in awe. I don't know what has become of her clique, but Arza's name no longer comes up. Every so often I hear her on the phone with a classmate named Michaela, that name is mentioned, but she doesn't visit Michaela's house and Michaela never visits ours. In fact, none of her friends does. When I ask about it, she shrugs it off. No particular reason. Hasn't even noticed. She lets me hold and kiss her like I used to. She cries softly sometimes, and when I stroke her forehead, she nuzzles into me. We have survived it.

Where her mood so easily soured before all this, it now seems to have steadied. She harbors no resentment against me and is not angry. She doesn't silence me when I speak.

When the first round of draft notices sends her classmates into a tizzy, she informs Meir and me plainly that she will not be enlisting. She will go see the military psychiatrist, get a discharge, and go travel. I'm surprised Meir doesn't make an issue out of this, and when I demand that he talk to her, he says, let her be. He says, that girl needs space. She'll go off and she'll heal.

Heal? Heal from what?

Let her be, Yoella, Meir repeats, and his voice is hard. And then, this time softly, he says, Yoli, let it go.

After Meir's death, after the shiva and the thirty-day mourning period, on the night before she was about to set off again, the two of us sat down at the dinner table. All those years she had wanted us to eat together as a family, wanted Meir to sit with us too, wanted Friday night dinners, and we tried, we'd sit down together, but we didn't understand how to generate the mass, maybe three is just too few for a family. Meir would have the TV on in the background. "It's the weekend news." But he had no interest in the news, and we'd eat quickly and get up, disbanding with lighthearted banter; in small families, one member's silence is enough to spoil everything.

I'd made us omelets and salad. Herbal tea in a teapot. Toast from the bread she liked. Meir was dead for five weeks now, thirty-five days had gone by since the funeral, and the days that froze in limbo flowed again. Meir was dead. Leah understood perfectly, perhaps quicker than me. It was now just the two of us.

During those weeks she'd left the house very little. Two or three times she visited my mother, met Yochai for lunch once, and once drove into town to run errands. I'd go into her room, hoping to find something in the closet, it didn't matter what, but she left everything piled on the chair. On top of the duffel bag. On the floor. She had taken to reading again. A book or two was always tossed on the bed or beside it.

I asked if she'd like more tea. Enough sugar? She smiled gently. Treated me softly. She spoke as little as possible during those days. Later I thought it was to protect me.

I said, "I'm so sorry."

She leveled her gaze at me.

"I didn't know how," I said. "I didn't know how to help you."

She looked at me a moment longer before bringing the mug to her lips again, and I thought, she understands what I'm saying, she understands.

"Are you all packed?" I blurted out. "Or can I help you pack?"

"Thanks," she said, "it's all right." She was always a gentle child, a gentle young woman. "It's okay, Mom."

Early the following morning I drove her to the airport. The next time I saw her, she was already twenty-eight years old and I was standing outside her window in Groningen, across the street.

56.

We're sitting in the car, Meir behind the wheel, me in the passenger seat and our animated daughter in back. I turn the radio to an upbeat song that spreads out among us and we happily hum along, getting the words wrong together. I place a loving hand on Meir's thigh and smile at Leah, her image fluttering in the car mirror. My daughter's mouth does not sink, and in fact, I cannot imagine anything that could mar her beauty.

"I've got a joke for you," Leah says. She's ten, and has recently taken to telling jokes. "Two hunters are walking in the woods, and suddenly—one of them collapses. Splat! The other guy calls an ambulance: 'Help! My friend is dead! What can I do?' And the operator says, 'Take a deep breath, I'll help you. First, let's make sure he's dead.' The guy goes silent for a moment, then the operator hears a shot. The guy gets back on the phone. 'Okay,' he says, 'now what?'"

Meir and I laugh.

Our daughter, in the back, is beaming.

I see all the peculiar ways in which mothers prepare their daughters for life, and they are always suffused with sorrow. My mother did not tell or ask or explain, but she acted, did not leave things to chance, and neither did I.

I remember finding my mother in my bed in the middle of the day. I came home and there she was, sleeping off a night shift. I also remember a time she got into my bed after I fell asleep, and when I woke up she whispered, shhh, shhh, sleep.

I remember this, this happened, and yet I wish there was someone else to ask, to eliminate doubt.

I remember the things I disclosed about Leah. I know what I meant. It matters, to understand what happened and to be able to explain and describe the things themselves, without the memory work that is forever at play. But I worry about the things that are inaccessible to me, that perhaps pull the rug out from under my stories, the things that elude me, the thousands of days that fused in my head inextricably, the mesh of gray matter. Because there were also the nights-upon-nights and days-upon-days. There were the thousands of wake-ups. The errands. The meals. The shopping. The thousands of hours of talk. And yet only seldom does something new resurface, pulling away from the other things and casting itself before me in sharp relief.

After my father died, my heart broke for him because I realized he never took up any space. He used to lie supine with his hands pressed against the sides of his body, and always seemed surprised when I asked for his opinion. He would say, no need, don't trouble yourself. I'm not thirsty. I already ate. He always said, here, take my seat. Of course I knew he was a mathematician, but I wasn't quite sure what he did all those years in his office at the university, and it was only after his passing that it occurred to me how odd it was that he had no students or teaching obligations of any sort. When I asked my mother about this, she said, it didn't work out, they left him alone. And only then did it dawn on me that I should feel sorry for her too. I mean, to be loved by a man like that? She was all by herself.

We didn't have many visitors at the shiva. My mother was touched by the doctors who showed up—she sat bolt upright in their presence. Her coworkers, nurses on the internal ward, all rallied around her. They took care of the hot water dispenser, the refreshments, the chairs. The neighbors trickled in. My classmates, the homeroom teacher and counselor too. It was strange to see them outside of school, on our couch, in our home, as if the curtain had been drawn back to reveal something they had been hiding about themselves that I was now forced to observe. I felt dazed, trapped between the two worlds, as if I'd been sleepwalking and woke up in the middle of a party.

My mother's doctor friend came to see us right after the funeral. I was sitting in my room with a few classmates when she walked in and staked a claim to our lives. "This cutie here I've known since the day she was born," she announced to the room. The following morning, she came again to help prepare the house for the consolers, opening pastry boxes and arranging chairs and trays. "All you need to do is sit," she told my mother and me. She didn't have children, she had a rabbit, and a month after my father's death she asked if I could come feed him for a week while she was abroad. Only twice a day, she said, and let him out of his cage for an hour each time, let him roam the house. She had a new TV set and a VCR, and would explain exactly how to use everything, I could hang out and enjoy the good life. "What do you say, Esther?" she asked my mother. "It's over Passover break, it'll give the kid a little something to do." And again she turned to me, tightening her grip, and said, "You'll have the house all to yourself, you can poke around," and cackled.

For a whole week I went to her house every morning and evening. I filled the rabbit's food bowl and freed him from his cage to hop around the house, trying to lure him onto the couch and into my lap. With my earnings I was planning to buy a pair of dangling gold earrings I'd seen at a shop downtown. The doctor returned from her trip with her cackling laughter and a fancy box of chocolates wrapped in a bow. She said, "This is from me, a thank-you gift. I'm so grateful, honey. Did you have a nice time in my house? Got some peace and quiet away from your mom?" It took a few more moments for me to realize she had no intention of paying me. "You're a good girl," she said, "a good daughter to a good woman."

At home I showed my mother the fancy chocolates. I remember her immediately saying, without a moment's hesitation, "That's very kind of her."

I read about Elaine and Cordelia years before Leah comes along and vow never to forget them. I only recently managed to escape my youth, pull through my problems, and now Elaine's story can tell me about myself. What really happened. I decide to remember Elaine and Cordelia always and know what to watch out for. But I don't think about the daughter I'll have, perhaps it doesn't occur to me to want one, perhaps I have even said to this or that person, not everyone should have kids, I have no intention of having kids.

Elaine and Cordelia are taking the *streetcar* to town. The writer doesn't describe Cordelia's smiles or how she wields them, she hasn't weaponized them yet, but her stare—Cordelia *can outstare anyone,* and Elaine is *almost as good.* They are thirteen years old, and across the distance of years, I think, it will seem to Elaine that they didn't know much about love; but they knew all right. *Our mouths are tough, crayon-red, shiny as nails,* she recalls. *We think we are friends.*

The day after I saw him at the gas station I came home earlier than usual. I had a migraine, left for the studio in the morning but headed back an hour later, wanting to rest at home. The phone rang in the living room, the landline; I'd almost forgotten that was an option. Who calls someone at home these days? No one calls people at home, not in the daytime, who's calling? The ringing reverberated violently in my ear, intrusive, destructive.

"Hello?"

But I knew right away it was him. Of course I knew. And he said, "She lied." He said my daughter lied and that I knew she was a liar and that he begged her to recant and she told him, my mother won't let me. He said my daughter and her friend had ruined his life. "Your daughter," he said. But he didn't say her name even once. "Your daughter and her friend" is what he said. They ruined his life. And then he said the one thing he was happy about, truly only one, was that he'd never have to see any of us again.

57.

L eah called," I tell Art. "She's arriving in two days with the girls. I'm going to see them."

Art knows—it is written all over his face—he knows that I have known for days, and that I should have told him right away, and why didn't I. But he does not ask, there is nothing to ask.

He asks, "Are you okay?"

I'm scared, but I also want this more than anything in the world.

"I'll be okay," I say, "yes."

I explain to Dr. Schonfeler that the disease draws the patient in, it's a collaboration, a partnership.

He seems interested. Tell me more, he says.

Imagine a rock scooped out by a giant explosion, I say.

Yes.

Imagine trying to open a jar. Force isn't enough, precision is just as important. But once you've opened it—the next few times it's easy.

I understand, he says.

From the moment the window of the disease opens, you can't close it again. Not really, not all the way. And you learn to hide it, that's the long labor of illness. That window might never open again, but the possibility is always there. The possibility is a disease of its own. From now on, you are always checking. You draw near the window, touch the hinges. You feel for the faintest draft. You're not sick but you're waiting for the disease. It is entirely possible that it, or something resembling it, will never happen to you again, and yet it keeps happening all the time. This is life on the verge. The soul has gotten tangled up, and even if you work out all the knots, each one of them, nothing will untangle you from the wait.

The house is always clean and tidy but now I look at it with different eyes, like I used to when my mother would visit and I knew she would notice the slightest smudge; suddenly, I see it too. And that's another mistake, because what I should do now is revert to a much earlier scrutiny, and open my childhood eye. What will my granddaughters see when they arrive? What do they know about me and what do they think and what has their mother told them? They know a little Hebrew and a little English. Dutch girls. But they are two, and that will help. They will remember this for each other. Years from now, they will be able to ask each other, do you remember? Did that happen? To resolve the contradictions together.

When my granddaughters are here, I want them to feel that the house is weightless. I change the sheets in the bedroom, the electric toothbrush heads and towels in the bathroom. My hairbrush lies in the bathroom drawer, its heavy conch handle and metal bristles, a brush that is neither innocent nor clean and that worries me now when I look at it. As a child I would come across crescent fingernail clippings or dirty laundry on our bathroom floor, or find myself standing in front of the open medicine cabinet. Discovering your grandmother's hair ensnared in metal spokes can be harrowing, anything indicative of the body's wear and tear, aging and sickness. I pluck the brush clean and put it back in the drawer but a moment later take it out again and place it somewhere else entirely, far from anyone's reach but my own. And then I sit in the living room and wait for the house to settle around me. I hear a dog bark and the hum of an air conditioner. A vacuum cleaner. Dripping water. Buzzing light bulbs. But from where? When Art's asleep beside me I can better identify the sources of sounds. On the street outside the window I hear a father ask his daughter, "Can you tell me why you're crying? Why? Why are you crying?" He doesn't give her time to answer. Every casual conversation passing outside my window conveys more information than I care to know. Despite the heat, I get up and close the windows.

Acknowledgments

I would like to express my immense gratitude to Deborah Harris, my incredible agent, who, with her wonderful team, has navigated—and walked me through—this fascinating journey.

Thank you so much:

Daniella Zamir, the marvelous translator of this novel into English.

Rebecca Saletan at Riverhead, an editor so brilliant and so reassuring.

Rebecca Servadio at London Literary Scouting, and Anna Carmichael, Sandy Violette, and Felicity Amor at the Abner Stein literary agency, for all your attentiveness and care.

I'm delighted to be published in English by Riverhead in the US and Bloomsbury in the UK. At Riverhead, I want to thank Catalina Trigo, Gretchen Achilles, Grace Han, Helen Yentus, Randee Marullo, Joy Simpkins, Claire McGinnis, Kitanna Hiromasa, Nora Alice Demick, Jynne Dilling Martin, and Geoff Kloske. At Bloomsbury, I'm especially grateful to Alexis Kirschbaum, who so warmly took my novel into her care, and to Stephanie Rathbone, Francisco Vilhena, Amy Donegan, Ros Ellis, Helen Upton, Cristiana Caserini, and Carmen R. Balit.

ACKNOWLEDGMENTS

——

Thank you, T, from the real-life Groningen, for traveling with me around my imagined Groningen.

Always—always—to Yigal Schwartz, my phenomenal teacher, editor, friend: Thank you.

And special thanks to my special darlings:
  Tami, Lilou, and Rocha, my dream team of early readers.
  Mom and Dad—where can I begin?—for everything.
  My beloved Kuki, for her enormous support.
  Gilad, my new guy for the past twenty-five years, hunk in shining armor, my one and only, my midlife teenage crush.
  My daughter, my precious, my sun. I love you so much.

Author's Note

Upon writing the fictional Yoella, I had come to entrust her with my own reading-life. I wish to express my deep reader's gratitude to those writers whose works surface in Yoella's thoughts throughout the novel, works that have deeply shaped my own literary consciousness. Their words appear in italics on the pages noted.

Pages 29–30, 35, 251: Margaret Atwood, *Cat's Eye* (New York: Doubleday, 1989; Anchor, 1998).

Page 5: Anne-Sophie Brasme, *Breathe,* trans. Rory Mulholland (New York: St. Martin's Griffin, 2004 and 2015).

Page 182: Phyllis Chesler, *Women and Madness* (New York: Doubleday, 1972; Chicago: Lawrence Hill Books, 2018).

Page 91: Roddy Doyle, *The Woman Who Walked into Doors* (New York: Viking, 1996; Penguin Books, 1997).

Page 3: Anne Enright, *The Gathering* (New York: Grove Atlantic Black Cat, 2007).

Pages 107–109, 114: Alice Munro, from the story "Silence," in *Runaway* (New York: Knopf, 2004; Vintage, 2005). In addition, on pages 117, 125, 197, and 216, the narrator's thoughts and speech are interspersed with unitalicized echoes of a quote from *Runaway*.

Page 210: Alice Munro, from the story "Child's Play," in *Too Much Happiness* (Knopf, 2009; Vintage Books, 2010).

Page 124: Heinz Frederick Peters, *My Sister, My Spouse: A Biography of Lou Andreas-Salomé* (New York: Norton, 1974).

Page 24: Susan Sontag, *On Photography* (New York: Farrar, Straus and Giroux, 1977; Picador, 2001).

Page 36: Elizabeth Strout, *My Name Is Lucy Barton* (New York: Random House, 2016).

Pages 105–106: Jeanette Winterson, *Why Be Happy When You Could Be Normal?* (New York: Grove Press, 2012 and 2013).

In addition, the dialogue between the characters on page 76 is interspersed with a quote and a paraphrase from Erich Kästner, *Dot and Anton*, trans. Anthea Bell (London: Pushkin Children's Books, 2015).